A FIC STINE
eart of the hunter
tine, R. L.
003000024970
TCHISON
010-09-02

ATCHISON, KS 66002

What's Happening to Me?

Jamie held out his arms. He could see his skin stretching, twisting, rolling up and down his arm as though something crawled beneath it.

He heard the sound of cracking bones. My bones, he realized.

Snap. Grind. Pop.

His nose pushed forward, growing longer and thicker. Forming a snout. Then thick hair sprouted across it.

His jaw tightened and moved against his will. His tongue rolled out. He felt his teeth become sharp and pointed.

He stared in horror at his hands. Thick black and silver hair burst through the skin covering his knuckles. The hair spread to cover the backs of his hands, his wrists, his arms.

His hands curled. His fingers shortened. His fingernails warping. Twisting into lethal claws.

Jamie growled low in his throat. His muscles stretched, and then grew tight. His shoulders hunched. His legs drew up beneath him. Stretching, straining, cracking.

A wolf! She turned him into a wolf!

ATCHISON LIBRARY
KANSAS

Books by R.L. Stine

Available from ARCHWAY Paperbacks

For orders other than by individual consumers, Pocket Books grants a discount on the purchase of **10 or more** copies of single titles for special markets or premium use. For further details, please write to the Vice-President of Special Markets, Pocket Books, 1633 Broadway, New York, NY 10019-6785, 8th Floor.

For information on how individual consumers can place orders, please write to Mail Order Department, Simon & Schuster Inc., 200 Old Tappan Road, Old Tappan, NJ 07675.

FEAR STREET SAGAS® #9
R·L·STINE

Heart of the Hunter

A Parachute Press Book

AN ARCHWAY PAPERBACK
Published by POCKET BOOKS
New York London Toronto Sydney Tokyo Singapore

The sale of this book without its cover is unauthorized. If you purchased this book without a cover, you should be aware that it was reported to the publisher as "unsold and destroyed." Neither the author nor the publisher has received payment for the sale of this "stripped book."

This book is a work of fiction. Names, characters, places and incidents are products of the author's imagination or are used fictitiously. Any resemblance to actual events or locales or persons, living or dead, is entirely coincidental.

AN ARCHWAY PAPERBACK *Original*

An Archway Paperback published by
POCKET BOOKS, a division of Simon & Schuster Inc.
1230 Avenue of the Americas, New York, NY 10020

Copyright © 1997 by Parachute Press, Inc.

HEART OF THE HUNTER WRITTEN BY ERIC WEINER

All rights reserved, including the right to reproduce this book or portions thereof in any form whatsoever. For information address Pocket Books, 1230 Avenue of the Americas, New York, NY 10020

ISBN: 0-671-00296-1

First Archway Paperback printing October 1997

10 9 8 7 6 5 4 3 2 1

FEAR STREET is a registered trademark of Parachute Press, Inc.

AN ARCHWAY PAPERBACK and colophon are registered trademarks of Simon & Schuster Inc.

Cover art by Lisa Falkenstern

Printed in the U.S.A.

IL 7+

ATCHISON LIBRARY
401 KANSAS
ATCHISON, KS 66002

Heart of the Hunter

Behind the
Iron Bars

Caged! Trapped behind iron bars.

He tried to slip through them. But the bars stood too close together.

He tried to bend them. But as hard as he pushed, the cold, solid metal held fast. Immovable.

I want to run, he thought. Fast. Like the wind during a storm.

I want to run quietly. Like a shadow over the ground.

He paced back and forth within the suffocating confines of his prison.

Escape! Escape!

The word echoed in his mind with each step. He circled the cell until he felt his head spin. So little room. His leg muscles ached with the urge to run.

He staggered to a stop. His silvery-blue eyes stared through the iron bars. He glared at the moon. Full and glowing. A perfect shimmering circle in the black sky.

Once it guided me through the darkness, he thought. But tonight it betrayed me.

He began to pace again. Faster. Faster. Thinking, remembering.

He shook his head. I don't want to remember. I don't want to think about the journey that brought me here.

But the memories were as strong as the iron bars.

He huddled in a corner. He covered his ears, but he still heard the long, wailing cries from his past.

He pressed his face against the iron bars, but he still smelled the blood. So much blood. Warm, rich . . . gushing.

He squeezed his eyes closed. But the horrible images still swirled before him.

I was young and innocent. I did not know enough to be afraid. I should have been terrified.

The memories carried him back to another time, another place.

Before he was a prisoner.

Before iron bars held him captive.

Before he knew what it was to fear.

Chapter
1

Kentucky Wilderness, 1792

Jamie Fier shifted his backside over the hard wooden bench. The wagon swayed. The wheels rumbled over the ruts and rocks in the road.

The Wilderness Road, they called it. Daniel Boone and others had carved it through the Cumberland Gap only two years before. Soon Virginia will be far behind us, he thought. But not soon enough.

He slapped the reins over the backs of the two chestnut horses. He was seventeen. Old enough to guide the wagon for his father.

The horses plodded along the narrow road that crept through the Appalachian Mountains. Jamie flicked his wrists again. The crack of the reins echoed around him.

"Patience, Jamie," his father scolded. He sat on the bench beside Jamie. "We can't go any faster than the wagon in front of us."

But I want to go faster, Jamie thought. The narrow road sliced through the mountains like a blackened tongue. He felt as though he were riding into the mouth of a beast. The tall pine trees looked like long, sharp teeth.

He knew the hungry wilderness could swallow them all. And they would never find their way out.

The thick canopy of branches overhead blocked out most of the sunlight. Wild animals could hide in the shadows, he thought. Watching. Waiting to spring onto the horses, onto me, onto Father. With sharp claws. Huge teeth.

Jamie shivered. The day was warm, but he felt clammy and cold. He pulled his flannel jacket tightly around him.

Two months ago, he had been so excited when his father announced that they were moving to Kentucky. A real adventure, Jamie thought. A new land. The unsettled frontier.

They could strike it rich there, beyond their wildest dreams, his father declared.

"I won't go, John. I won't go!" Jamie's mother had cried. "It's too wild. Too dangerous."

But she had packed her pots, kettles, and quilts into the wagon. She climbed into the back and started the long journey with them.

And she's sorry she did, Jamie thought.

One of their wheels struck a large rut in the road. The wagon jerked. Jamie heard his mother give a shrill cry.

"What was that?" she called out. "John, what's happening?"

His father turned his thin face slightly and peered through the slit in the canvas that covered the wagon. "Just a little bump in the road, Dora Mae. Nothing to worry about."

"John, please, let's return to Virginia," Jamie's mother begged.

Jamie cringed. Every day, she made the same request. And every time, his father gave the same reply.

"We were starving in Virginia," his father snapped. Then he returned his attention to the rough road.

Jamie glanced over at him. His silver-blue eyes—eyes like Jamie's—were narrowed to two slits. Jamie saw a muscle jump in his father's hollow cheek, just above his graying beard. Jamie knew his father's thoughts before he spoke.

"It's the Fier curse," his father mumbled. "I'm a good farmer, but the curse is like the plague. It stopped our tobacco crops from growing. We had nothing to sell—so no money to buy food."

His father dug his bony fingers into Jamie's knee. "You'll see, son. Things will be different now. We left the curse behind us."

Jamie had grown up hearing about the curse. How it doomed all the Fiers. How none could escape it.

Or so his father used to say. But now he promised that they *had* escaped it. Jamie didn't know what was true.

I won't believe in the curse, Jamie decided. I don't believe in the curse. Bad soil. No rain. Hot sun. Those are the reasons our crops failed. Not because of some silly family curse that began centuries ago.

He slapped the reins again, leaned forward, and planted his elbows on his thighs. Father thinks of little else besides this ridiculous curse. If he had spent as much time working the fields as he did worrying, our crops would have been fine.

Jamie stared at the wagon ahead of him. He noticed a small hole in the canvas flap that covered the back opening. He stared at the hole, hoping Laura Goode would peek out.

Jamie saw a flash of blond hair appear in the hole. He straightened, wet the tips of his fingers, and slicked down his black hair.

Laura was the most beautiful girl he'd ever seen. Every day he tried to position their wagon behind the Goodes' so he could catch a glimpse of her. She had long blond hair that flowed down her back. Her eyes were as green as the leaves on the branches overhead.

A girl peeped through the hole. But it was Laura's sister, Amanda. Amanda was fifteen, a year younger than Laura. She wore her blond hair parted down the middle and braided on each side. Bright red bows secured the ends. Her brown eyes reminded Jamie of mud.

She waved at him, her hand flapping wildly in the air. Jamie didn't wave back. What a nuisance, he thought. Always following me around the camp, telling me how much she likes me.

Amanda pressed her fingers to her lips. Then she held out her palm and blew. Blew a kiss to him.

Jamie rolled his eyes. She is so childish. So silly. I hope Laura doesn't think I like Amanda, he thought.

Not that he had a chance with Laura anyway. Her father and his seemed to hate each other. They'd barely exchanged a civil word.

Jamie had never known his father to take such a strong dislike to anyone as he had to Lucien Goode. But his father's hatred of the man wasn't without reason, Jamie reflected.

From the start, Goode had proven himself to be selfish, lazy, and prone to lying. He slept through his turn on the night watch, and more than once he'd positioned his wagon ahead of the Fiers' when it had been the Goode family's turn to take the last position for the day. The last wagon was most vulnerable to attack.

And once when a scout returned with fresh meat, the Fiers had missed out on their ration. But Lucien Goode had walked away with double his share. Jamie's father confronted the man, and the two had nearly come to blows. Yes, there was good reason why his father hated Lucien Goode.

Ooooowwwooo!

The long, high-pitched howl made the hairs on the

back of Jamie's neck prickle. Was that a wolf? he wondered. He tensed, waiting for the sound to come again.

Ooooowwwoo!

Is it as close as it sounds? he wondered.

Ooooowwwooo!

Close. Too close. It's watching us, he thought. His gaze darted over the trees, and his fingers tightened around the leather reins.

He looked at Amanda. Her eyes had grown as round as full moons.

Maybe it wasn't an animal at all. Maybe Indians were calling to each other. He knew they could imitate animal cries.

Do Indians live in this part of Kentucky? he thought. He had heard the stories of Indians capturing settlers, taking them prisoner, using them as slaves. He knew the Shawnee did not want settlers coming to Kentucky.

Thump.

Jamie jerked in his seat and fought to keep his balance. Something had bumped into the wagon.

What was that? he asked himself. He leaned over and checked the side of the wagon nearest him.

Nothing there.

Did a tree branch hit the wagon as we passed?

Or is it the Indians? Are they sneaking in for an attack?

We're moving too slow, Jamie thought. Anyone—anything—could climb into the back of the wagon and we'd never know. Never know until it was too late!

He snapped the reins. But the horses did not speed up. The wagon continued to roll along slowly.

Thump. Bump.

The sound came from inside the wagon, he realized. His heart thundered.

"Father, did you hear—" Jamie began.

"Jamie, look out!" Amanda shrieked, pointing her finger. "Look behind you!"

Jamie jerked around. And stared into the black open barrel of a flintlock rifle.

A rifle aimed straight at his heart.

Chapter
2

Jamie stared openmouthed at his mother. She stood behind him, holding the loaded rifle in shaky hands. Pointing the barrel straight at his chest.

The rifle glinted in the late day sun. Jamie didn't dare breathe. He didn't dare blink.

"Dora Mae! What in the world do you think you're doing?" Jamie's father demanded. He jerked the rifle from his wife's grasp.

Jamie pulled a ragged breath into his lungs. She pointed the gun at me. At her own son!

"I heard a wild animal," his mother choked out. Jamie saw her eyes fill with tears. She dug her trembling fingers into Jamie's arm. "Jamie, tell your father to take us home."

He cleared his throat, trying to make his voice sound firm. "I want to settle in Kentucky."

Tears trailed down his mother's cheeks. She turned to Jamie's father. "We'll find nothing but sorrow here. You can't escape the curse, John. It's in your blood. It's in Jamie's blood." She returned to the back of the wagon.

Jamie's father laid the rifle behind their feet. "Probably a good idea to keep the rifle handy," he whispered. "Those wolves sounded close."

"Do you think it might have been Indians?" Jamie asked softly, so his mother wouldn't hear.

His father snorted. "Indians wouldn't attack this many people. We're safe."

I hope so, Jamie thought.

"We're pulling off the trail now," his father said. "Stay close to the Goodes' wagon. I don't trust them."

Jamie said nothing. He didn't want to encourage his father to talk about Lucien Goode. But his father started anyway.

"That Lucien Goode," his father said. "As poor an excuse for a man as I've ever seen. A lying, conniving, low-down cheat. Greedy hog. Doesn't know what it is to be without. Now he's running low on water and I've seen him eyeing ours."

Jamie's father reached down and patted the rifle. "I think your mother was wise to ready this."

They reached a small clearing. Jamie knew the routine. The wagons followed each other until they formed a small circle. It gave them a little protection during the night.

Jamie guided their wagon into position. Then he climbed down and hurried around to the back. He looked inside. His mother was huddled in a corner, shaking.

"Why have we stopped?" she asked.

"It's evening. We've stopped for today." He held out his hand. "Come on, Mother, you need to fix supper."

"Supper," she repeated. She crawled to him. "Yes, yes, I must fix supper."

Jamie helped her out of the wagon. She squeezed his hand, worry filling her eyes. "I don't like this new land," she whispered harshly. "Too many shadows."

"Once we reach the valley, the shadows will disappear," Jamie assured her.

His mother smiled. "You are such a good boy, Jamie." She gently touched his hair.

He wanted to remind her that he was almost a man, but she wandered away before he could speak. *Sometimes I don't think she realizes that I am grown,* he thought.

"Just crackers tonight," his father ordered.

Father is rationing our food too much. Jamie glanced around at the other families. *No one else is as stingy. I've lost so much weight that I'm surprised my britches haven't fallen to my knees.*

He watched his father unharness the horses and tether them to a nearby bush. Jamie grabbed two feed bags full of oats from the back of the wagon and brought them over to the horses.

No matter how little I get to eat, the horses have to

be fed, he realized. Jamie slipped a feed bag over each horse's head, anchoring it behind their ears. They munched the oats greedily.

"Jamie! Jamie Fier!"

He turned quickly at the sound of the excited voice. Amanda Goode hurried to his side. "Jamie, why didn't you wave to me this afternoon when I waved at you?" she asked, pouting.

"I'm sorry, Amanda. I thought you were shooing flies away," he lied.

She giggled. "Oh, Jamie. You're so funny." She grabbed his arm. "I was so frightened when I saw that rifle poking out of your wagon. I thought you were going to be killed right then and there. Whatever was your mother thinking? All you had to do was hit a bump in the road and bang! No more Jamie Fier!"

He jerked away from her. "My mother thought she heard wolves."

Amanda's brown eyes widened. "I think it was Indians," she whispered. "Once we had an Indian servant. She told me fascinating stories. So many unbelievable things . . ."

Amanda prattled on about the Indians, telling him everything she knew. Jamie stopped listening. I really don't care, Amanda, he thought.

He took a step away from her. "If you'll excuse me, I have chores to do."

"I can help you, Jamie. I don't have any chores tonight."

Jamie sighed heavily. "Amanda, I'd really like to be alone."

She ignored him and kept talking. "Papa's worried we'll never reach the settlement. We're almost out of food. If the scout doesn't come back soon with good news, Papa doesn't know what we'll do."

"I'm sure the scout will return soon," Jamie said. "Kentucky is filled with wild game."

"That's what everyone says. But where is the game? We haven't seen one deer. Not even one rabbit!" She flung her arm in a circle. "Papa says the journey is cursed. What if he's right?"

"He's not," Jamie said angrily. If I hear the word *curse* one more time, I think I might be sick, Jamie thought.

"But what if the scout doesn't return? Or what if he hasn't found anything?" Amanda asked. She grabbed his arm and shook him as though that would make him understand her words. "Jamie, we'll all starve to death!"

"We're not going to starve," Jamie scoffed. "We have plenty of food left."

"You do," she answered. "But we don't. Our supplies are almost gone. I think Laura might have to boil dirty socks to make a stew tonight."

"Amanda!"

They both spun around at the sound of the sharp voice. Laura stood a short distance away. She planted her hands on her hips and frowned at her sister.

Laura is so beautiful, Jamie thought. Why can't I ever think of anything to say to her?

"Papa and I are hungry, Amanda. You need to stop dallying and come cook supper," Laura scolded.

"It's your turn to prepare the food tonight," Amanda replied. "I'm going to help Jamie with his chores."

Laura ran her fingers across her forehead. "But I feel one of my awful headaches coming on. I must lie down. Please wake me when supper is ready." She turned back toward the Goodes' wagon.

"Is she really sick?" Jamie asked. He wanted to help Laura back to her wagon. But he felt too shy to offer.

"She's delicate and tires easily," Amanda explained. She smiled brightly. "Once she fainted during dinner. Her face fell into a bowl of soup. It was so funny."

Jamie heard excited yelling coming from the wagons. "The scout must be back," he told Amanda.

He dashed to the camp, Amanda right behind him. A huge fire burned brightly in the center of the circle of wagons. The writhing flames cast an eerie glow over the men gathered around it. But the scout wasn't in sight.

"We have to do something!" Lucien Goode yelled. "The scout hasn't returned. My children are hungry!"

"Give him another day," Wagonmaster Thomas urged. "We can't be that far from water and game. He's bound to return tomorrow with good news."

"He's dead!" Lucien cried. "He's been gone four days! He must be dead."

Jamie noticed several men nodding their agreement. The women looked frightened. The little children hid behind their mothers' skirts.

"This journey is cursed!" Lucien yelled. "We

should have arrived at the settlement by now, but wagons have broken. Game is scarce. If we want to reach the settlement alive, we must take drastic action."

"What sort of action?" a man asked.

Lucien spun around and pointed a finger at Jamie's father. "The Fiers are cursed. I've heard him say so. Their curse has tainted us. All of us!"

Lucien took a menacing step toward John Fier. His eyes glowed brightly as he glared at Jamie's father. Jamie could see the fire's flames reflected in their dark depths.

"I say we take the Fiers' food and leave them and their curse behind!" Lucien shouted. "I say we leave them to die!"

Chapter
3

"Noooo!"

Jamie heard his mother's horrified cry. His own heart pounded so hard his ribs hurt.

"You can't leave us to die!" Jamie yelled.

No one paid any attention.

"We should leave them behind!" a woman declared.

"Won't share their food," a gray-haired man muttered.

Everyone who was gathered around the fire began to talk at once. Their voices grew louder and louder.

"Won't part with a bite of food. Not one single scrap!" someone shouted.

"I heard John Fier complaining to his wife that the

family was cursed," a woman told the group. "He said his family has been cursed for generations."

"We're not cursed!" Jamie protested. "We've been rationing our food. That's the reason we have more. If you rationed—"

He heard the sound of metal scraping against wood. He spun around and saw his father pulling the loaded flintlock rifle from the wagon.

Jamie's father slapped the rifle butt into the crook of his shoulder and pointed the long barrel at Lucien Goode.

"Just try to take my food," his father dared him. "Just try and I'll show you the curse of a bullet."

Threatening them isn't the answer, Jamie realized. "Father?" he called.

His father jerked his head toward Jamie. His eyes glittered savagely. Jamie's breath lodged in his throat.

Jamie swallowed hard. He made his way to his father's side. "Father, I believe Wagonmaster Thomas is right. I think the scout will return soon. Surely we could share our food with our traveling friends tonight."

"No!" his father bellowed. "This is our food, our water."

Jamie heard a twig snap. He glanced around. The men circled them, gathering close. Their eyes fixed on his father.

"Give us half your food," Lucien demanded, his eyes blazing with fury. "And we'll let you travel with us."

Say yes, Jamie thought. I don't want to travel alone. Not in the wilderness. We won't stand a chance. If the wild animals don't get us, the Indians surely will.

"Please, Father, let us share," he urged.

"No!" his father cried. He raised the rifle to eye level.

But it was too late. The men had moved closer. So close.

"Then we'll take it," Lucien yelled.

The men rushed at Jamie's father.

"No!" Jamie cried. He leapt at Lucien Goode.

The man threw him aside. With a jarring thud, Jamie hit the ground. His head slammed against a wagon wheel. Pain burst through his skull. Red lights flashed before his eyes.

The world teetered and spun. From far away, he heard a woman gasp. "Jamie, are you all right?" a voice asked.

He struggled to focus. He saw Amanda kneeling beside him and felt her fingertips moving over his head.

"I'm fine," he growled. He shoved her hands away. He scrambled to his feet, but his legs buckled. He tumbled back to the ground.

He saw that the men had grabbed his father and were trying to wrestle the rifle from his grasp.

His father twisted one way, then the other, clutching the rifle. He fought to shake Lucien and the other men off. He still held the gun tightly in his fingers.

Lucien swung Jamie's father around. Jamie saw his

1 9

father's face twist into a fierce, ugly grimace. He saw his father struggle to aim the rifle barrel straight at Lucien Goode's chest. But Lucien held the barrel tight with two beefy hands.

An explosion ripped through the air.

And a woman uttered a long, shrill scream.

Chapter
4

Jamie's mother clutched her chest and crumpled to the ground. Father's rifle went off. He accidentally shot Mother! Jamie scrambled to his feet and rushed to her side. Then he dropped to his knees beside her.

Crimson blood soaked the front of her dress. The glistening pool grew wider and wider.

"What have they done? What have they done to you?" Jamie cried.

He pressed his hand over the gaping black hole in her dress. Her blood gushed through his fingers.

She clutched Jamie's shirt and pulled him nearer. He watched her fight to draw air into her lungs. She struggled to speak. Her mouth opened and closed. Bright red blood bubbled past her lips.

"What? What, Mother?" Jamie cried.

She gagged and gasped. Her body jerked in his arms. Once. Twice.

Then she stilled. The blood continued to trail from the corner of her mouth in a tiny rivulet, but she no longer tried to speak. Her eyes glazed over. Her fingers released their hold on Jamie.

"Nooo!" Jamie's father uttered an anguished cry.

Jamie snapped his head up. Lucien Goode held his father by the shoulders. His father tore himself away from Lucien and rushed to Dora Mae's side.

He shoved Jamie aside, knelt, and gathered his wife in his arms. He began to rock back and forth. Back and forth.

"It's all right, Dora Mae," he whispered. Tears coursed down his cheeks. "It's all right."

But Jamie knew his father lied. It was too late. It would never be all right.

His mother's eyes gazed up, but she saw nothing. Her mouth hung open, but she did not speak. Like a child's rag doll, her arms and legs hung limp and motionless.

She was dead.

Jamie heard an excited shout and the sound of pounding hooves. The scout galloped into the camp. "I found water!" he cried as he reined in his horse. "A mountain spring. Less than a half day's ride!"

Jamie looked back at his mother. He touched his finger to her cold cheek. She doesn't need water or food anymore, he thought sadly. All she needs now is a grave.

The days after his mother's death rolled past as slowly as the wagons. Jamie began to wonder if they would ever reach the settlement.

"We'll have a log cabin, Dora Mae. With three rooms." Jamie stiffened at his father's words. He held his breath when his father turned slightly on the wagon seat and peered into the back of the wagon.

"Would you like that, Dora Mae?" his father asked. He paused. He tilted his head to one side as if listening for an answer. "I knew you would," he said.

He turned back around and dug his hard, bony fingers into Jamie's arm. He leaned close to him. "Your mother is so easy to please," he whispered.

Because she's dead! Jamie screamed inside his head. She's dead!

But his father seemed to have forgotten. All day, all night, he talked to Jamie's mother as though she still traveled in the wagon.

He's gone insane, Jamie thought. He knows his rifle killed Mother. He knew she never wanted to leave Virginia.

"What sort of furniture should we make for your mother?" his father asked.

Jamie closed his eyes and swallowed hard. Mother doesn't need furniture, he thought.

His father described the dresser he would build. He continued to talk to Jamie's mother as they stopped for the night. He talked to her during supper.

When Jamie and his father bedded down in the wagon, his father made Jamie say good night to her. Jamie hated it when his father made him speak to his mother. He wanted to shake his father and yell at him. She's dead, he wanted to scream.

But a son should honor and respect his father. Jamie pulled his blanket higher around his shoulders and tried to sleep. But he couldn't.

The huge fire in the center of the camp sent shadows dancing over the outside of the canvas. Jamie watched them. Wondering. Worrying.

What am I going to do? It's bad enough that Father talks to me as though Mother is alive. But lately, he's started talking this way to the other travelers as well. I overheard him telling the wagonmaster that Mother is tired of the journey.

He invited Lucien and his daughters to share a meal with us when Mother is feeling better. Lucien Goode. A man Father hates and despises.

Will Lucien tell the others what Father said? Has he been talking behind our backs? Making people suspicious of us? Whispering about the curse? Telling everyone that Father is mad?

Jamie noticed that the people had begun to keep their distance from him and his father. Some had hinted that the Fiers shouldn't be allowed in the circle of wagons.

And we're so much safer when we are part of the group, he thought.

Jamie's father began whimpering softly in his sleep.

Jamie silently tossed his covers back and crawled across the wagon. He climbed out. He could see clearly in the small glade. A crescent moon hung in the black sky. Stars glittered above.

The camp stood in silence. He saw two men walking the perimeter. Watching and waiting for Indians, Jamie thought. The deeper they traveled into Kentucky, the more the group feared an attack.

Jamie crept toward the forest. He needed to be alone. *What can I do about Lucien Goode? He has so much influence over the others. If he wants us out of the group, the others will listen.*

Lucien Goode. He despised the man. He watched Lucien when no one was looking. Watched and plotted his revenge.

Lucien wanted to leave us to die, Jamie thought. *He killed my mother.*

Jamie stumbled to a stop. He hadn't been paying attention to where he was going. He now found himself deep in the woods. The night shadows surrounded him.

Shafts of moonlight pierced the thick boughs overhead and shimmered over the ground.

Swoosh!

An owl swept down from the treetops, its wings spread wide. Jamie ducked. He felt the rush of air as it flew past him.

He heard a long, lonesome wail whispering through the trees. A wolf? he wondered. Or just the wind?

A cold chill skittered along his spine. He rubbed his

arms for warmth. He heard the breeze knocking the boughs of the trees together. His mother's words, a low lament, circled him on the wind.

The curse is in your blood. You cannot escape it!

But he would. Somehow he would. He wondered how fast, how far he would have to run to escape the curse.

What was that? Jamie held his breath and listened. Something rustled in the brush. Then silence.

Jamie shivered. I'm not alone, he realized. What's out there? Is it an animal? Or the Shawnee?

Why didn't I think to bring the rifle? I have no way to protect myself.

He heard someone softly call his name. "Jamie! Jaaamieee!"

He spun around. A figure all in white drifted toward him. "Jaamieeee . . ."

A woman. Glowing in the moonlight. Trailing white robes. Her long hair loose around her shoulders.

"Mother!" he cried.

Chapter
5

Jamie's blood pounded in his temples. He staggered backward.

"Mother?" he called again. He didn't dare take his eyes off the white figure. He watched as it stumbled, then righted itself.

Stumbled? A ghost wouldn't stumble, would it?

He peered through the shadows. Amanda! Amanda followed me. The moonlight reflected off her long white nightgown.

"I saw you leave the camp," she whispered as though she thought someone might overhear her. "I remember when my mother died. I couldn't sleep for months."

"My mother didn't die," he snapped at her. "Your father murdered her."

"*Your* father shot her," Amanda replied. "He never should have picked up the rifle." She held up her hands. "Not that I blame him. You shouldn't blame him either. It just happened."

"Your father tried to steal our supplies," he reminded her.

"Oh, Jamie, let's not talk about this," Amanda exclaimed. "I came to warn you."

He narrowed his eyes. "Warn me about what?"

She moved nearer. She glanced around the forest before she answered him. "Do you think we're safe here?" she whispered. "I feel like eyes are in the trees watching us."

"If Indians were watching, they would have attacked by now," he scoffed. "What did you come to warn me about?"

She gave him an uncertain look. She took another step closer. "I overheard the men talking," she confided, her voice low. "Some believe the rumor that your father is cursed. They fear the curse will spread to them."

Jamie snorted. "A curse. The only curse is brought on by their greed," he said. But he felt his stomach knot.

"Some have heard your father talking to your mother." Amanda grabbed his arm. "Jamie, they want to leave you behind!"

Rage surged through him. "They think that's the

answer? To leave us at the mercy of savage Indians and wild animals?"

"The Indians aren't savages, Jamie. I told you an Indian woman worked as our servant for a while. She was very kind. She taught me so many wonderful things. If the Shawnee should find your father, they would treat him with respect because of his age," she said. "And they wouldn't hurt you. I'm sure of it."

"I bet your father is the one who wants to leave us behind," Jamie accused. "I bet he's trying to talk the others into the idea."

Amanda bowed her head. "I'm ashamed to admit it, but yes, he's urging the others to leave you behind," she answered in a hoarse voice. "All the talk frightens me. I don't want them to leave you alone."

She lifted her gaze to his, and her fingers tightened around his arm. "Marry me, Jamie. If you're my husband, he'll have to take you with us."

"Marry you?" Jamie choked back his laughter. "You're the last girl in the world I'd ever want to marry, Amanda," he replied harshly.

He heard Amanda draw in a sharp breath. She didn't say anything for a long moment.

Maybe she finally realizes I don't want anything to do with her, Jamie thought.

"Don't you think I know by now how you feel about me, Jamie?" Amanda replied in a harsh whisper. "I'm not stupid, you know."

"I never said—"

"I know you don't love me," she cut in, "but maybe

you shouldn't bother worrying about love right now, Jamie. This is a question of life and death. Marry me and you'll survive. I think your choice is clear," she added.

Her smug tone sickened him. "And what of my father?" Jamie asked.

She lowered her gaze again. "I'm sorry, but we can't help him. If he is indeed cursed—"

Jamie jerked free of her grasp. "Well, I don't want to be your husband. I hate you. I hate your father. I hate your whole family." He started to stalk away.

"I love you, Jamie! Marry me!" she cried.

He spun around to face her. "Never!" Jamie vowed. "Your father is the reason my mother is dead. He's the reason my father is slowly going mad. He's ruined every hope my family ever had for a new life. I'll get even with Lucien Goode if it's the last thing I do!"

Chapter
6

Jamie stared down the mountain. The valley below was lush and green. A paradise.

It took us two days to get this far, he thought. And the valley is still so far away.

The wagons began descending the mountain. Jamie waited until the Goode wagon had traveled a considerable distance ahead, then he urged the horses forward.

They whinnied and strained. Then the wagon began to roll. Jamie could see the horses' muscles relaxing.

Going down a mountain should be easier than going up, he thought. The wagon started to rumble.

The wheels turned fast, faster. He could see the horses growing agitated. Nervous.

"Slow down!" his father yelled.

The wagon is going to roll faster than the horses can run, Jamie thought. We're going to ram into the Goodes, he realized. We'll be killed!

Jamie wrapped his hand around the brake handle and pulled back, trying to slow the wagon before it rolled over the horses.

Crack!

Was that an axle? he wondered frantically. Or a wheel?

The horses whinnied.

The wagon started to teeter.

"Jump, Jamie!" his father yelled. "Jump, Dora Mae!"

Jamie leapt for the side of the mountain. He hit the hard ground with a thud. His father landed a few feet away.

Jamie heard the grinding sound and another snap. A wheel spun away from the wagon. The wagon crashed on its side and came to a dead halt. The wheel continued to roll and bounce along the side of the road.

"The axle," Jamie's father muttered. "The curse is still with us. Dora Mae is right. We can't escape it. We are doomed!"

Jamie staggered to his feet. He held his hand out to his father and pulled him up.

"I'd better check on your mother. She didn't jump

when I told her to," his father mumbled as he trudged to the wagon.

Jamie squeezed his eyes shut. Oh, Father, what am I going to do with you? How can I make you realize Mother is dead?

The other wagons stopped and Jamie heard excited voices. He opened his eyes. People approached their wagon. He slowly walked over to them.

"What happened?" Lucien Goode asked.

"I think our axle broke," Jamie said wearily.

The wagonmaster got down on his knees and looked under the wagon. "It split right down the middle. You won't be able to repair it quickly," he told Jamie.

"Then we'll have to leave them behind," Lucien Goode declared.

The wagonmaster stood. "I don't like to leave people behind. Especially on this side of the mountain. The Shawnee hunt along here."

"Which is exactly why we can't wait for them," Lucien stated flatly.

"I agree that we can't wait," the wagonmaster said. "Someone will have to take the Fiers into their wagon."

Jamie looked at the people gathered around him. He studied each face, staring into each pair of eyes. One by one, their blank, cold gazes dropped to the ground. No one offered their wagon to him or his father.

"Well?" the wagonmaster roared.

Jamie waited.

"The Fiers are cursed," someone finally said. "I don't want them in my wagon."

"Neither do I," someone else admitted.

The others only mumbled and muttered, but Jamie understood only too well what they thought. What they felt. Lucien Goode has convinced them that my family is cursed, he realized. He has convinced them all!

"We don't need you, anyway!" his father bellowed.

Jamie jerked around at the sound of his father's harsh voice. His father jabbed his bony fist in the air. "Go on. Leave us! None of you ever talk to Dora Mae anyway."

Jamie felt a warm hand slip into his. He snapped his head around and glared at Amanda.

"Come with us, Jamie," she pleaded. "Your father has lost his mind. Leave him and come with us."

"Never!" Jamie spat. "Your father is our curse!"

"Leave him alone, Amanda," Laura Goode urged. She tilted her nose into the air. "Father wouldn't let him travel with us anyway."

Jamie stared at Laura. Why did I ever think she was pretty? he wondered. At least Amanda worries that I'll be left alone. Laura only cares for herself.

The people shuffled away. The wagonmaster turned to Jamie. Jamie read a mixture of sympathy and fear in his expression.

"I'll slow them down as much as I can. Maybe you

can fix the wagon quickly and catch up. Just stay on this road. Don't take any detours," he warned.

Jamie watched him walk away. They've cast us aside as though we had the plague, he thought.

Forsaken us.

Deserted us.

"Good riddance!" his father called. "You were just slowing us down."

Jamie watched the wagons roll along the road. Roll away from him. Away from him, his deranged father, and their broken wagon.

That night Jamie huddled beside a small camp fire. A long tree branch lay across his lap. He peeled off the bark with his knife.

I should be able to use this to replace the axle, he thought. If we only lose a day, we might be able to catch up with the others. The horses are strong. I could lighten the wagon. Leave Mother's belongings here so we could travel faster.

A wolf howled into the pitch-black night.

Jamie froze. His father did not even glance up. He continued staring at the fire.

Did Father hear the wolf? Jamie wondered.

Suddenly his father stood. "Dora Mae? Yes, dear, I'm coming."

Jamie jumped to his feet and grabbed his father's arm. "Father, don't go into the woods. I heard a wolf."

"Your mother is calling me," Jamie's father insisted. "I must go. She needs me," he muttered as he ran into the shadows.

Jamie dashed after him. He stumbled on a rock and fell. He shoved himself to his feet and looked around frantically. He could no longer see his father's outline in the darkness. He could only hear the distant sound of his father's footsteps crashing through the leaves and brush.

"Father, stop!" he called. He cupped his hands around his mouth and called louder. "Come back! Please, I can't see you anymore, Father. You must come back!"

He's not coming, Jamie realized. He stood silently, listening for his father's footsteps. He heard nothing.

The damp night air soaked his clothing, chilling him to the bone. Jamie shivered. He hugged his arms around his chest for warmth.

Maybe he won't wander too far, Jamie thought. Maybe he won't stay long when he realizes Mother isn't hiding behind the trees.

Jamie returned to his seat by the fire. He spotted the pouch that held his ammunition and tied it to his belt. He picked up the horn that held his powder and slung it over his shoulder. He positioned his rifle by his feet.

Then he took up his knife and continued whittling the new axle. The blade scraped away the rough bark. *Scrape. Scratch. Scrape.*

The fire crackled. A loud pop sent a shower of

glowing red embers into the night. Jamie jerked back.

He heard a long, high-pitched scream pierce the darkness.

His father. What could have made his father scream that way?

Chapter
7

"Father!" Jamie cried.

No answer.

He dropped the branch and slipped his knife into the sheath at his side. He snatched up the rifle and a lantern, then dashed into the woods.

A thick mist floated between the trees. Jamie could barely see a single step ahead of him.

"Father?" he whispered hoarsely. "Father?"

No answer.

Where could he be? Jamie lowered the lantern to the ground. He could see pine needles and twigs smashed into the earth. Father must have come this way.

He followed the trail. Slowly. Cautiously. Listening hard.

The lantern swayed. The light jumped around the forest. It flashed on the trees. The ground.

On his father's twisted body.

Jamie's heart pounded. Slowly he moved closer. The light from the lantern cast a yellow glow over his father's face. His father's eyes never blinked. They just stared. His mouth hung open as though he were still screaming.

His throat had been torn away to reveal glistening blood and snow-white bone.

Jamie felt burning bile rise into his throat. He swallowed hard.

What did this? he wondered frantically. His vision blurred with burning tears. He swiped them away with the back of his sleeve. What killed my father?

A wolf?

A bear?

Indians?

He heard a long, high-pitched howl. It could be a wolf or Indians. They used animal cries to call to each other.

Jamie's gaze darted around the woods. His breath came in small gasps. He inhaled the rusty smell of his father's blood. If I can smell it, animals will surely smell it, he thought wildly. I can't stay here.

He began to run back toward the camp. Tree branches snagged his clothes. Twigs snapped beneath his feet.

His legs pumped furiously. His breathing grew louder. I have to get away from here. Run! Run!

He spotted a flickering light through the trees. The camp. He would be safe there, but for how long?

Not long enough, he thought. I'm alone. All alone now.

He rushed into the camp. He dropped to his knees, gasping for breath. Everything looked the same.

But something was wrong.

He could feel it in his bones.

What's wrong? he wondered. What's different? He slowly looked around the camp.

The branch he'd been whittling stood where he had left it. The fire continued to burn. The wagon still lay on its side.

The horses!

He stood up, scanning the area. The horses! The horses were gone.

He set the lantern on the ground. With shaking hands, he pulled the ramrod from the rifle and jammed it down the barrel. Then he poured gunpowder from the horn into the barrel. He knew too much powder would make the rifle explode in his face when he pulled the trigger, but he didn't have time to measure it out.

"Please don't be too much," he whispered to himself. "Please don't be too much gunpowder."

He opened his pouch, removed a small metal ball, wrapped it in a tiny piece of cotton, and popped it into his mouth. When he had covered it with spit, he rammed it all the way into the barrel.

He glanced around. He could hear nothing but his own breathing, his own heart thundering. He could see nothing but the dancing shadows created by the fire.

He put a small amount of powder in the flash pan of the rifle and pulled back the hammer, locking it into place. Now he only had to pull the trigger.

He turned slowly, studying the trees. I'm so stupid, he suddenly realized. They can see me in the firelight, but I can't see them.

He rushed into the shadows and crouched beside a tree. Maybe the horses broke free. Maybe no one took them, he thought. Father tied them. Maybe he forgot to put a knot in the ropes.

Yes, yes, he thought, trying to calm his breathing. That's what happened. They broke free. And a wolf killed Father. With one bullet, I can kill a wolf. Then I can reload.

Always keep the rifle loaded, he told himself. Always be ready to fire it.

He glanced over his shoulder. He could see the road in the pale moonlight. If he walked fast, he could catch up with the others. If no one will share their wagon with me, I'll walk the entire way, he decided.

I just don't want to be alone.

He stood and peered intently into the darkness until his eyes burned. He saw nothing moving.

I won't walk on the road, he thought. The moonlight is my enemy on the road. It will make me visible. I'll walk through the forest that lines the road. I'll be safe in the shadows.

He darted through the trees and began to walk. Quickly. Quietly.

He heard a noise and stopped to listen. What was that? he wondered. Footsteps?

He heard branches rustling in the breeze. Nothing else. He began to walk in long strides.

Again he heard something—a whisper in the trees.

Ooooowwwooo!

The hairs on the back of his neck prickled.

Ooooowwwooo!

Is it the wolf that killed my father? Is it stalking me now?

He walked faster.

Something leapt from the tree in front of him and landed with a soft thud.

An Indian!

Chapter
8

Jamie staggered back. He tripped over a rock and fell. His rifle fired. His solitary bullet flew into the night sky.

He scrambled to his feet. I don't have time to reload, he thought frantically. I don't know if I *could* reload in the dark.

He grabbed the barrel of his rifle and held it like a club. Waiting. Waiting for the Indian to attack. His mouth grew dry. He had never seen an Indian before.

Blue lines trailed across the Indian's forehead and down his cheeks. The sides of his head were shaved bare. A strip of short hair ran down the center. Feathers were knotted in it. A necklace of pointed teeth circled his neck.

The Indian warrior dropped his head back. *"Ooooowwwooo!"*

He sounds just like a wolf, Jamie realized. Indians *were* making the animal cries. They've been following us for days.

Should I turn around and run back to the wagon? Or should I run in another direction? To the left? To the right?

The warrior howled again. Jamie heard a thud behind him. He spun around.

Another Indian!

He heard a sound to his left. Then his right. More Indians. They surrounded him.

His feet froze to the spot. His knees felt like the slippery mud that lined a river. His heart raced, fast and hard. He could almost hear it in the thick silence that filled the forest.

He began to sweat. The rifle became slick in his palms, sliding through his hands.

The warrior curled his lips in a smile of triumph. His white teeth shone in the moonlight.

Terrified, Jamie yelled and swung his rifle at the Indian in front of him.

The other Indians moved quickly. Silently.

A rope cut into Jamie's legs. He tripped and fell to the ground.

An Indian snatched the rifle from his hands. A warrior grabbed his legs. Another grabbed his hands. Jamie struggled and fought, but he soon found his hands bound with a leather strip that bit into his wrists.

He rolled back and forth, kicking. "No! Get away!" he cried out. He heard the desperate sound of his voice echo in the darkness. Useless, Jamie thought. Who could hear him? Who would help?

A cold leather band circled his neck. He felt it tighten with a quick jerk.

Another jerk. Tighter. He stopped struggling. He lay perfectly still. Waiting.

Laughter echoed between the trees. Another jerk tightened the noose around his neck until it dug into his throat, cutting off his air, suffocating him.

He gagged. His throat burned. His chest ached.

He brought his bound hands up. He scratched and clawed at his neck, trying to loosen the circle of leather.

But it only tightened more. He thrashed frantically, wearing himself out.

His hands fell limply from his throat. His body jerked and grew still.

A red haze filled his vision and the truth slammed through him.

I'm going to die!

Chapter
9

The leather noose loosened and air rushed into his mouth. Jamie rolled to his side, gagging and coughing. He drew more of the warm night air into his aching lungs.

Jamie felt someone grab his shoulder and haul him to his feet. He stared at his captor. The Indian grinned, baring large teeth. The whites of his large, dark eyes seemed to glow in contrast with the blue streaks on his face. The muscles of his bare arms and shoulders looked taut and powerful.

His gaze locked on Jamie's. The Indian tugged the long strip of leather that was tied to Jamie's hands. His body jerked forward and fell and he heard the other Indians surrounding him laugh.

Jamie stood up and yanked on the leather strip. The Indian's expression darkened. He swiftly reached out and shoved Jamie. Jamie stumbled back to the ground.

"What do you want?" he asked as he staggered to his feet.

The Indian began to walk, tugging on the leather strip around Jamie's neck, giving him no choice but to follow—like a dog on a leash.

They walked to a clearing where the Indians' horses were tethered. The Indians mounted and set out through the woods, Jamie trotting to keep up.

They traveled all night. As the first light of dawn filtered through the trees, Jamie's eyes drifted closed. He fell to the ground for what must have been the tenth time since the ordeal began. But he had no urge to get up again. His body craved sleep.

He felt the Indian tug on the leather lead, but Jamie kept his eyes closed. He didn't move a muscle. He heard his captor walk toward him and felt the Indian's leather-covered toe dig into his ribs.

Jamie groaned and rolled over. A few moments later, water splashed on his face. He sat up and the Indian handed him the leather sack of water. Jamie drank greedily.

Too quickly, the water was taken away. The Indian handed him a strip of dried meat. Jamie sniffed it and felt bile rise in his throat. It smelled foul.

The Indian yelled at him. Jamie shook his head. He didn't understand.

The Indian grabbed a handful of Jamie's hair with

one hand and pushed the meat into Jamie's face with the other. Jamie held his breath and forced himself to take a bite.

He held the meat on his tongue for an instant and felt his stomach convulse. The meat tasted like rotten fish. He spit it out.

The lump of half-chewed meat landed on his captor's foot. Jamie heard the other Indians roar with laughter and watched his captor's face turn dark with fury.

The Indian tightened his grasp on Jamie's hair and pulled him up to his feet. Jamie gritted his teeth. He felt his hair being pulled out by the roots.

Finally, the Indian released his hold. Jamie's head flopped forward. He saw the Indian remove a large leather sack from his horse's back.

The Indian pressed the sack to Jamie's chest, then quickly lashed it to his body with long leather strips. Jamie inhaled an unmistakable, utterly putrid smell. The meat. The sack held an entire load of the revolting meat. They set off again.

Jamie felt smothered by the disgusting smell. He tried to hold his breath. Finally, he gasped for air, his nose and mouth filling with the horrible, rank odor.

Each time Jamie's steps slowed, his captor pulled him forward. The sack tied to his chest felt heavier and heavier. Inside his heavy boots, his feet felt like two swollen lumps of flesh.

When night came, the Indians stopped once. They gave him water. They laughed as they pulled chunks of the dried meat from the sack and waved fistfuls of it in his face.

All too soon they began to move again. Every muscle in Jamie's body burned. He didn't think he could walk one more step. But he had no choice.

Dawn came again. Jumbled, ragged thoughts and images ran through Jamie's exhausted mind. The same questions echoed in his head. What will they do with me? Will I be a slave or will they kill me?

He gazed up at the hot sun, glowing in a clear, blue sky. A wave of dizziness swept through him. Then total blackness surrounded him.

When his eyes opened again, he saw the ground passing below him, and the slow-stepping hooves of a horse. He lifted his head and realized he'd been slung over a horse sideways. He saw the Indians who had captured him.

One of the Indians ran ahead toward a clearing in the woods. Jamie heard the Indian's shouts ring out and then heard other shouts in answer.

The horse stopped and his captor pulled Jamie down. His legs shook as he forced himself to stand up. He looked up ahead at the clearing. He saw smoke rising from open fires and low huts made of leather and bark.

An Indian camp, Jamie thought. As they entered the camp, a group of children ran toward him. They laughed at him and poked him with sticks. The adults gathered in small groups, staring and talking.

I don't understand their language, but I'm certain they are talking about me, Jamie thought.

His captor led him into a bark-covered hut. Inside, an old woman turned away from the fire. Her hair was streaked black and white. Her face was wrinkled like a raisin.

The Indian tugged on the leather band around Jamie's neck and said something to the woman. She hobbled across the hut and gazed deeply into Jamie's eyes. Then she trailed one of her gnarled fingers along his cheek. He shuddered.

"You have the eyes of a wolf," she rasped.

Jamie stared at her. "You speak English!"

"My father was a fur trader. He spoke English," the woman replied. "My mother was a Shawnee. I am called Withering Woman."

"Why do they call you that?"

"Because I have always looked old," she told him. "And I have always been wise. This tribe is the lost Shawnee. We are separate from the main tribes. We go our own way."

She said something to the man holding his leash. He unsheathed a large knife. Jamie held his breath, wondering what the old woman had said, what the warrior would do to him.

The Indian cut the leather that bound his hands. Then he removed the noose from around Jamie's throat. Jamie took a deep breath.

"That is Running Elk. He is our chief," Withering Woman said.

Jamie nodded at the man. Running Elk narrowed his black eyes.

Withering Woman crooked her finger. "Come. Sit

by my fire." She sat on the ground, her legs crossed beneath her. Jamie dropped down beside her.

He glanced over his shoulder. Those who had captured him stood by the door, their arms crossed over their bare chests. "They have never seen eyes such as yours," the old woman explained.

She took his hand. Before he could stop her, she picked up a knife and slashed it across his palm.

He cried out and tried to pull free, but her bony fingers dug into his wrist. Running Elk grabbed his shoulders and held him in place.

Withering Woman held his hand over a bowl. His crimson blood slowly dripped into it. *Drip. Drip. Drip.* Filling the small bowl.

When the bowl was full, Withering Woman dropped his hand. Jamie cradled it against his chest. What does she want with my blood? he thought.

The old woman smacked her lips. She carried the bowl to her mouth and tipped her head back.

No, Jamie thought. She's not going to drink it. She can't. He felt his stomach churn.

Withering Woman gulped down the blood. Twin rivulets of red ran down either side of her chin.

She moved the bowl away from her mouth and smiled, her teeth stained with his blood. "You are the one," she rasped. "The one we have been waiting for."

Chapter
10

"You are the one!" she repeated with conviction.

Jamie stared at the old woman, her words echoing around him. *I am the one they have been waiting for?* He shook his head. "What are you talking about?" he asked.

"Once we were never hungry," she said. "Buffalo roamed the land. But now our people have been unable to find them. We are starving."

What does this have to do with me? Jamie thought. But he remained silent.

"One night I stared into the fire and had a vision," Withering Woman continued. "I saw a boy with eyes such as yours. I knew he would lead us to the buffalo. You are the one we have been waiting for."

"I don't know anything about tracking buffalo," he told her.

"It doesn't matter. You are the one." She took his arm and pulled him to his feet. "Come. You must prove your worth."

Jamie realized all the warriors had already left the hut. They are so quiet, he thought. So swift.

He followed the old woman outside. Immediately, he saw an Indian girl about his own age. She wore her shiny black hair in two long braids. A brown buckskin dress covered her slender body. Strings of shiny black and red beads circled her neck. She turned her head slightly. Their eyes met.

Jamie's breath lodged in his throat. She had such smooth, dark skin. Deep, dark eyes. And she was so delicate and graceful.

She made him forget that he had once thought Laura Goode was beautiful. He could not take his eyes off her. "Who is that?" Jamie asked.

"Whispering Wind," the old woman told him. She shook his arm. "You must prove yourself."

He swung his head around and stared at her. "What?"

"You must run the warrior's gauntlet." She pointed one gnarled and crooked finger.

Jamie glanced over . . . and froze.

The Shawnee men had formed two long rows, six feet apart. They had smeared fresh war paint over their faces. Feathers dangled from their heads. Their chests were bare. Their muscles looked hard as rocks.

The warriors stomped their feet. They threw their heads back and howled. They swung clubs, switches made from branches . . . and tomahawks.

The tomahawks glinted in the sunlight as they slashed through the air. The keen-edged blades would slash through his skin just as easily.

"You must run through the warrior's gauntlet," the old woman repeated. "Or they will kill you!"

Jamie stepped back. "Don't you think those weapons will kill me?"

"Not if you are the true one." With two fingers, she pointed to his eyes. "Watch them with your wolf eyes. Run swiftly."

Jamie's heart thundered. He cast a sideways look at Whispering Wind. She no longer watched him. She watched the warriors, smiling at them.

He wanted her to look at him. He turned to Withering Woman. "What do I do?"

"Remove your shirt and boots. Pretend you are a wolf. Run fast," she urged. "Very fast."

A wolf, Jamie thought. How am I supposed to do that?

He jerked his shirt over his head. He dropped to the ground and removed his shoes. He heard soft laughter.

He snapped his head around. Whispering Wind pointed at his shoes and giggled. She wore shoes of soft animal hide. His shoes were hard.

If I survive this ordeal, I will make Whispering Wind stop laughing. I will make her look at me with respect.

He stood. Drums began to beat.

Boom. Boom. Boom, boom, boom. Boom. Boom.

He felt rivulets of sweat dripping down his body. His mouth grew dry. His heart pounded in his chest, matching the beat of the tribal drums.

"Like the wolf," Withering Woman reminded him. "Run fast."

Run fast, Jamie repeated to himself. Run fast.

The drums beat louder.

The pounding filled his head.

The warriors threw back their heads and screeched. Then they fell silent and stared at him. Daring him. Daring him to run through the gauntlet.

Jamie took a deep breath. He rushed into the gauntlet of warriors.

He ducked a tomahawk and felt a switch lash his back. But he did not stop.

Run. Run fast. Run swiftly.

The words echoed in his mind.

Duck. Twist. Crouch. Run.

The tomahawks fell faster. Slicing through the air.

Swish. In front of him. *Swish.* Beside him.

He dropped to the ground and rolled. Then he

scrambled to his feet and ran. He gasped for breath.

Sweat poured into his eyes. He saw the end of the line through a red haze.

I'm going to make it, he thought. I'm going to make it.

Running Elk leapt in front of him. He raised his tomahawk, his dark eyes glittering.

A wolf, Jamie thought. Move like a wolf.

He lowered his head and lunged at Running Elk. He butted into the warrior chief and sent him sprawling to the ground.

Jamie staggered to his feet. He leapt over Running Elk and raced past the last warriors. He wrapped his arms around a tree, trying to catch his breath, trying to stop his shaking. His legs felt rubbery. His body trembled from his efforts.

But he had escaped the gauntlet! He pushed himself away from the tree, spun around, and raised his arms over his head in victory. "I did it! I did it!"

Whispering Wind ran toward him, a concerned expression on her face. I impressed her, he thought. She knows how brave I am now.

She glared at him and fell to her knees beside Running Elk.

Jamie felt his victory slip away. Panting heavily, he leaned against the tree. Suddenly, he felt tired again. Drained. Exhausted.

He glanced down. Cuts, scratches, and gashes covered his body. Blood stained his pants crimson in dark, expanding patches.

He watched his blood flow faster, faster. As fast as he had run. Darkening the ground at his feet.

He looked up. The warriors circled him, moving closer. Closer.

Chapter
11

———

Pain. Jamie's senses screamed with pain. He lay on his back, unable to move. Everything hurt. Even his eyelids felt bruised and swollen. They ached as he struggled to open his eyes.

He saw shadows dance eerily over bark-covered walls. Where am I? he wondered. What am I doing here?

"Good. At last you are awake."

Jamie jerked his head to the side at the sound of the raspy voice. He saw an old woman tossing something that looked like dried leaves into the flames of an open fire—

He remembered everything in a flash. Shawnee! Captive! Warrior's gauntlet!

I must have passed out, he realized. I lost so much blood.

He gazed at his chest. His cuts were covered with a black, sticky mess. He touched the stuff with one fingertip. "What is this?" he asked.

Withering Woman turned from the fire. "Medicine. It will heal your wounds. And the magic powder I just tossed into the fire will take the burning from your skin."

Jamie released a sigh of relief. "Then I'm not going to die."

"You impressed the warriors," she told him.

But not Whispering Wind, Jamie thought. I did not impress her.

"They will vote soon," Withering Woman told him.

Groaning, Jamie sat up. "What do you mean 'They will vote soon?'"

He heard a yell outside the hut. "It is time," Withering Woman said. "Come. We will learn your fate."

My fate? Jamie wondered. Must I run the warrior's gauntlet again? I'm too weak and battered. I wouldn't stand a chance this time.

He wished he had listened to Amanda's prattle about Indian customs so he would know what to expect.

His legs trembled as he stood. He followed Withering Woman out of the hut. Night had fallen. A sliver of a moon shone in the black sky. A huge fire burned brightly in the center of the camp. Red sparks shot into the night, bursting, burning, dying.

When Withering Woman and Jamie reached the fire, the warriors formed a circle around them. One warrior held a brightly painted wooden club. He passed it to the warrior beside him.

"He has voted life," Withering Woman told him.

The next warrior threw the club to the ground.

Withering Woman dug her fingers into Jamie's arm. "He has voted death," she said in a low voice.

Death! They are voting on whether I live or die, Jamie realized.

The next warrior picked up the club and threw it back to the ground.

Death!

The warrior beside him picked it up and passed it to the next warrior.

Life.

Life.

Death.

Life.

Death.

Jamie lost track of the count. How many voted for life? How many voted for death? His hands curled into fists. He gritted his teeth to keep from yelling out.

But I ran the gauntlet! he wanted to shout. I ran it and I survived.

The warriors continued to pass and throw, pass and throw the club until it reached the last warrior— Running Elk.

"What is the vote?" Jamie asked Withering Woman.

"Even. Twenty-five for life. Twenty-five for death. Running Elk will cast the deciding vote."

"Then I am doomed," Jamie muttered quietly. He remembered the anger in Running Elk's eyes when Jamie spat the piece of meat on his foot. He remembered the fury in the warrior's face when Jamie knocked him to the ground.

Running Elk locked his black gaze on Jamie. The other warriors stood silently as they waited for their leader's vote. The only sound Jamie heard was the roaring fire.

Jamie held the warrior's gaze. He wanted to look away, but he had to see the final vote. He had to know if death awaited him.

Running Elk passed the club to the warrior beside him. Relief swamped Jamie. He fell to his knees and bowed his head.

Life!

They are going to let me live, he thought.

He glanced up at Running Elk. But for how long?

Chapter
12

———

Running Elk gestured for Jamie to return to Withering Woman's lodge. The old woman nudged him forward. He entered the hut and sat before her fire.

The warriors followed. They filed into her hut and stood along the walls, their arms crossed over their chests.

What now? Jamie wondered. He glanced around at their stony expressions. He swallowed a lump in his throat.

Withering Woman squatted in front of him. She poked her fingers through his hair as though she were looking for lice. Suddenly she yanked a strand free by the roots.

"Ow!" Jamie cried. He rubbed his scalp. "What are you doing?"

"I must prepare you for the ceremony." She leaned forward and whispered in his ear. "Be still. Think only of life. If you offend them, they may take another vote."

He raised his gaze to the warriors. Running Elk glared at him. In order to survive, I must become one of them, Jamie thought.

He nodded at the men. He forced himself to remain expressionless and still. Withering Woman slowly pulled out his hair, strand by strand. He bit down on his tongue to keep from crying out.

He forced himself to think of something else. Anything else. To show his pain might be asking for death.

He stared at the fire. He saw Whispering Wind. She turned toward him. She smiled and held out her hand.

Withering Woman pulled hard on a tuft of hair. At the stinging pain, the lovely image vanished.

In its place, the image of Lucien Goode rose up in the flames. Jamie imagined Lucien Goode's face consumed by the fiery tongues. Slowly burning. Utterly destroyed. He nearly laughed out loud.

Yes, I must do everything I can to survive, he thought. I must live to have my revenge on Lucien Goode.

"There. You are almost ready," Withering Woman said. Jamie touched the sides and the back of his head with his fingertips. He felt only bare skin.

I'm like a chicken plucked for dinner, Jamie thought. Withering Woman took the hair that remained along his crown and braided beads through it. Then she rose to her feet. "We go now," she said.

Jamie stood. I feel so naked with no hair, he thought. "Where are we going?"

"To the great council house," she said.

Running Elk led the way to a long wooden structure. Jamie noticed that the image of a wolf was painted on the door. Running Elk opened the door and pointed for Jamie to go inside.

Swallowing hard, he obeyed. Benches lined the walls. Women and children stood at the far end of the hut. Jamie glanced over his shoulder. The warriors had not entered.

Each woman walked up to him and gave him a gift. Clothing. A beaded sheath for his knife. Flint and steel for building a fire. A tobacco pouch.

Whispering Wind approached him last. She walked slowly, her eyes downcast. She stopped before him and held out a pair of moccasins.

Jamie smiled, wishing he knew how to speak Shawnee. "Thank you," he said. She backed away.

"Sit!" Withering Woman ordered. Jamie knelt on the bearskin near the fire. He watched the warriors enter the council house and sit in a circle along the walls. Holding a pipe, Running Elk sat in front of Jamie.

He reached around Jamie, took a twig from the fire, and lit the pipe. He placed it in his mouth.

Silence filled the hut. The smoke curled and spiraled toward the ceiling. Running Elk offered the pipe to Jamie.

Jamie had once smoked tobacco on the plantation. He knew to inhale only a little bit or he would go into a coughing fit. He brought the brightly painted pipe to his lips and took a small puff. Then he handed it back to Running Elk.

Running Elk nodded. "It is done!" Withering Woman announced. "You are now Shawnee."

The days passed quickly for Jamie and his respect for the Shawnee grew. He began to understand their language. He wore deerskin britches like they did. A fringe ran the length of his long legs. In his moccasins, he learned to move silently, like a shadow, through the forest without leaving a trail.

Every morning, Running Elk painted Jamie's face and chest for wisdom and for luck. Every day they searched for the buffalo. Every evening they returned to the village with nothing.

One night Running Elk stopped Jamie before he could go into his hut.

"Where are the buffalo?" Running Elk demanded. Jamie had learned enough of the Shawnee language to understand him.

"They are near," he replied.

Running Elk narrowed his eyes in suspicion. "If you speak falsely, you will die."

Jamie watched Running Elk walk away. He didn't

know what would happen to him if he didn't find buffalo soon. That's why they let me live, he thought. They thought I was the boy from Withering Woman's vision—the one who could lead them to the buffalo.

But I'm not. I can't be. And they are going to find out.

Jamie heard laughter. He turned and saw several women rolling a wooden ball across the camp, using only their feet. Men were trying to stop them.

Everyone laughed and shouted. It's a game, Jamie realized.

Suddenly he felt very alone. He wanted to join them. But he didn't feel welcome. I live with the Shawnee, but I am not truly Shawnee, he thought sadly.

Every day he spoke to no one but Running Elk and Withering Woman. Every morning and evening Jamie ate his meals with Withering Woman and every night he slept alone in his own hut.

The group ran closer. He watched a warrior work the ball away from a woman and begin to push it to the other side of the camp. Whispering Wind dashed after the warrior. She moved in front of him and skillfully kicked the ball away from him.

She smiled and began to roll the ball back to the side of the camp where Jamie's hut was. Mesmerized, Jamie watched her. He felt his loneliness grow.

She glanced up from her rapidly moving feet and looked at Jamie. I wish I weren't the outsider, he thought. I wish they would let me play with them. But they never did. They did not fully trust him.

Whispering Wind kicked the ball hard. It rolled toward Jamie and stopped near his feet. He stared at the ball. Then he looked up at Whispering Wind. She smiled shyly and waved him over.

Jamie glanced at the other players. One by one, each motioned for him to join them. Gladness filled Jamie. He lightly kicked the ball and watched it roll over the ground. Then he kicked it a little harder and scrambled after it when it took an unexpected turn toward the forest.

He heard laughter, but it didn't sound mean. He felt a hand on his arm. He glanced up. Whispering Wind watched him.

"Do your people not play?" she asked.

Jamie was grateful he had learned a little of the Shawnee language. "No, I've never played this game," he told her.

"Watch," she ordered. She put the side of her foot against the ball and shoved it. It rolled back toward the camp.

"So I should use the side of my foot and not my toe," Jamie said.

She smiled. "And still you will lose."

She kicked the ball again and ran back into the circle of players. We'll see about that, Jamie thought. He raced after her, taking his place with the warriors. They played for hours, until the moon rose high in the night sky.

Whispering Wind had spoken the truth. The warriors lost.

That night Jamie lay alone in his hut. Through a small hole in the roof, he watched the stars. He thought of Whispering Wind. She made him feel as though he belonged.

A black cloud passed over the sky. Jamie thought of Lucien Goode and the darkness he had brought to Jamie's life.

The Shawnee are teaching me a lot, he thought. A lot that I can use when I avenge my parents' deaths. I have learned to hunt and track so I can find Lucien Goode.

But I don't want to leave the Shawnee. I think I'm falling in love with Whispering Wind.

His eyes closed. Sleep overwhelmed him. Images of Whispering Wind and Lucien Goode filled his dreams. He could not have both. Love or revenge. He would have to choose one.

The next morning, the warriors greeted him with friendly words. Jamie knew their attitude had changed because Whispering Wind had invited him to play with them the night before. He was grateful for that.

The men seemed to believe more than ever that he was the one who would find the buffalo.

But I'm not, he thought.

Jamie held that secret close to his heart while he trudged through the woods with the warriors, searching for the sacred animal.

More days passed and they found no buffalo. The

warriors grew tense and restless. They stopped laughing with him. They stopped talking to him.

Jamie saw only suspicion in their eyes. They will soon realize the truth. They will soon realize I have no special powers.

Then they will kill me—without mercy.

Chapter
13

Tired and frustrated, Jamie returned to camp with the warriors. He felt hunger gnawing at his belly. He knew they did, too.

If only we would find the buffalo, Jamie thought, they would come to trust me. And maybe then, Whispering Wind would look at me the way she looks at Running Elk.

He spotted Whispering Wind sitting before her hut, her loom in front of her. He glanced around. He did not see Running Elk. He walked across the camp and crouched beside Whispering Wind.

"Hello, Whispering Wind," he said quietly in the language of the Shawnee. She smiled shyly at him like she always did, her nimble fingers weaving the threads through the loom.

"I have no blanket in my hut," he said. He rubbed the material she had woven between his fingers.

She shoved his hand away. "This blanket is for the warrior I will marry," she told him. "When I have finished weaving it, I will give it to the warrior I have chosen. I will become his wife."

"Give it to me, Whispering Wind," he said softly. "I will be a good husband."

She laughed. "Eyes of the Wolf, you cannot marry," she said. "You have no feathers to mark your bravery. A woman must choose the bravest of warriors to sleep in her hut."

She is right, he realized. I have no feathers. Only the scars that crisscross my chest and back. Scars I won running the warrior's gauntlet.

"Eyes of the Wolf!"

Jamie turned at the raspy voice. Withering Woman stood in the doorway of her hut. She motioned him over.

"Good-bye, Whispering Wind," he said quietly. She said nothing, but continued to work on her marriage blanket.

Jamie strolled to Withering Woman's hut. "Come inside," she whispered, her gaze darting past him.

He slipped into her hut. Shadows lurked in the corners. Jamie imagined he could smell old blood. Rank. Rusty.

"You have not found the buffalo," Withering Woman whispered.

Jamie shrugged. "I've hunted each day with the others. From dawn to dusk. Tomorrow perhaps we will meet the buffalo."

"Perhaps." Withering Woman nodded. "Or perhaps tomorrow night you will meet the end of your life."

"The end of my life?" Jamie moved closer. "What are you talking about?"

"The men do not trust you. They are talking of taking another vote," Withering Woman explained.

Jamie squeezed his eyes closed. Another vote. I won't stand a chance. They will vote to kill me this time.

He paced across the hut. Back and forth. "I'm trying, but I know nothing about the buffalo. I look for signs, but all I see is Whispering Wind. She is all I think about."

He dared to meet Withering Woman's gaze. "I am falling in love with her." He shook his head. "But she wants a brave warrior."

"I know magic that can help you," Withering Woman told him.

Jamie jerked his head up. "Magic?"

She moved her hands through the air. "A spell. A powerful spell. It will make her love you."

Hope surged through Jamie. "Use it. Use it to make her love me. I'll find the buffalo then."

Withering Woman narrowed her eyes and shook one of her gnarled fingers in his face. "Be certain, Eyes of the Wolf, that you want this power. Once done, it cannot be undone."

"I want Whispering Wind to be my wife," Jamie insisted.

"The price is high."

"I will pay any price to have Whispering Wind's love. Tell me, tell me what I must give you."

She answered in a low whisper. "When the moon is full, you must give me your soul."

Behind the
Iron Bars

My soul!

He looked at the bars of his prison.

She wanted my soul! Why did I agree?

He bolted from the corner where he had been huddling. He began to pace. Back and forth, the memories chasing him.

I wanted Whispering Wind for my wife. She was almost finished with her marriage blanket. I knew she would give it to Running Elk if I did not do something—soon. Something that would make her want to marry me.

I didn't even know what my soul was.

I couldn't feel it. I couldn't touch it. It seemed simple enough to give it away. To trade it for Whispering Wind's love.

He drew to a stop and glanced through the iron bars. Glared at the full moon. The full moon that had become his enemy.

I did not know of the full moon's power. Of its danger, he thought.

I waited, waited for it, anticipating the night when it would rise high in the black sky. For on that night, Withering Woman promised Whispering Wind would be mine.

Within his prison, he prowled, fast, faster.

The memories swirling.

I loved Whispering Wind. I wanted her to marry me. The old woman had been the only one who believed in me. Who never doubted me. I believed she wanted to help me.

Eyes of the Wolf, she had called me. Eyes of the Wolf, I became.

I made my choice. I would forget about Lucien Goode. I would stay with the Shawnee forever. I would take Whispering Wind as my wife and find happiness.

On the night of the full moon, I rose from my bed and followed the old woman into the forest.

If only she had told me everything.

If only I had known everything that waited for me deep within the woods.

If only I had known what would happen when the moon was full.

If only I had·known what it meant to give up my soul.

Chapter
14

Jamie followed Withering Woman deep into the forest. The cool night air chilled his bare skin. He watched the wind toss branches to and fro. He felt as if they might reach out and grab him. Drag him into the inky black night.

He fought the sudden urge to turn back. To turn and run toward the camp. To hide in his dark hut.

What magic would the old woman work on him? Maybe her spell would hurt him. Kill him.

He suddenly stopped walking. Frozen to the spot.

Withering Woman turned and stared at him. He felt as if she had heard his thoughts. He watched a slow smile curl her thin lips.

"Sometimes it is wise to fear, Eyes of the Wolf," she

said simply. "But now you have gone too far to turn back." Withering Woman dropped to her knees. "Come. Sit before me."

Jamie knelt, facing her. His buckskin britches kept his legs warm, but his bare chest was cold. "What are you going to do?" Jamie asked.

"Shh! You must remain silent until the ritual is over," she warned him.

When the ritual is over, you will have my soul, Jamie thought. Will it hurt to lose it?

The full moon shone into the clearing, casting its silver light over Withering Woman. She removed a strip of leather from around her neck. Jamie could see that the leather was threaded through a hole she had drilled into a tooth.

"The tooth of a wolf," Withering Woman whispered reverently. "A wolf is powerful. Smart. Fast."

She laid the tooth in her cupped palm. In the moonlight, Jamie could see a strange drawing carved on it—a claw, holding five circles.

Without warning, Withering Woman slashed the tooth across Jamie's chest. Jamie released a startled cry and jerked back. He saw drops of his blood glistening in the moonlight. Warm against his chilled skin.

Withering Woman dropped the leather strip around his neck. The tooth settled perfectly into the gash. Jamie thought he could actually hear his heartbeat echoing through the tooth. *Thump. Thump. Thump.*

Withering Woman took a leather sack and a small wooden bowl from her pouch. She poured the liquid from the sack into the bowl, dropped her head back, and drank. Then she handed the bowl to Jamie. "Drink," she ordered.

"What is this?" Jamie asked.

"It has the power to give you all you deserve. When next Whispering Wind gazes on you, she will fall in love with you," Withering Woman promised.

Jamie closed his eyes. He heard Whispering Wind's laughter. He saw her smile. Her long slender fingers weaving the colorful threads through the loom.

She finished her marriage blanket today, Jamie remembered. Tomorrow she will give it to Running Elk. After tomorrow, she will never be mine.

He brought the bowl to his lips. The smell of blood hit his nostrils. Whose blood? he wondered. It does not matter, if it will bring Whispering Wind to me.

Jamie let some of the thick, dark liquid flow down his throat. He gagged and coughed.

Withering Woman watched him. She pushed the bowl back up to his mouth. He drank the rest in one swallow. Then licked his lips, gathering the last of the drops.

"What now?" he asked.

Withering Woman smiled eerily. "We wait."

Her words sent a shiver up Jamie's back. But he forced himself to sit quietly. And wait.

Pain sliced through his stomach. He doubled over. "What did you give me?" he demanded, gasping for breath.

"Power," she growled.

Jamie felt his body grow freezing cold. Then burning hot. His fingers tingled and stung. Then his toes. Then his whole body.

He hugged himself in a tight ball. He gritted his teeth against the stinging pain. His body shook and trembled. He stretched out, facedown on the forest floor. Violent spasms raced through him. Faster and faster.

What's happening? he wondered. What's happening to me?

He held out his arms. He could see his skin stretching, twisting, rolling up and down his arms as though something crawled beneath it.

He heard the sound of cracking bones. My bones, he realized.

Snap. Grind. Pop.

His breathing grew faster. His heart pounded hard. His nose pushed forward, growing longer and thicker. Forming a snout. Then thick hair sprouted across it.

His jaw tightened and moved against his will. His tongue rolled out. He felt his teeth become sharp and pointed.

He began to pant, pant like a dog. He crouched on all fours. He tried to stand, but he fell back to the ground.

He rolled onto his back and stared in horror at his hands. Thick black and silver hair burst through the skin covering his knuckles. The hair spread to cover the backs of his hands, his wrists, his arms.

His hands curled. His fingers shortened. His fingernails warping. Twisting into lethal claws.

"No!" Jamie cried. "No!"

The words came out thick and garbled, his tongue and lips and throat no longer suited to human speech.

He rolled over. Again he tried to stand. Again he fell to all fours.

Jamie growled low in his throat. His muscles stretched, and then grew tight. His shoulders hunched. His legs drew up beneath him. Stretching, straining, cracking.

Changing what he was. Changing what he had always been.

He looked at Withering Woman and saw a reflection of what he had become.

A wolf!

Chapter
15

A wolf! Jamie's mind screamed. Withering Woman is a wolf too!

She turned me into a wolf!

He had to get away from her. Jamie began to run. Faster than he had ever run.

On padded paws. On four legs. Low to the ground.

His powerful legs churned beneath his body. He felt as if he flew through the forest. Barely touching the ground.

Quietly. Like an Indian. Like a shadow.

Like a wolf!

I can see through the darkness, he realized. My vision is sharper . . . all my senses are sharper. I can smell . . . smell the other animals.

I can smell the owl in the tree above and the ground mice scampering beneath the leaves. I can hear their tiny squeaks.

He did not know where he ran, he only knew that he had to get away.

Withering Woman lied to me! Tricked me! Whispering Wind will never love me now. She'll never fall in love with the animal I've become.

Why? Why did Withering Woman do this to me? What did she gain?

He leapt over a fallen tree without missing a step. And ran on. As fast as his four legs would take him.

He staggered to a stop at the edge of the mountain. His tongue hung from his mouth. Dripping saliva onto the ground. He rolled his tongue over his lips. He could feel his sharp canine teeth scrape against it.

He could see rich green meadows far below him. Like snakes, silver rivers wound through the fertile land. And the buffalo drank from the streams.

The buffalo. I found them! A thousand. Maybe more.

His ears pricked up. He listened—listened to the babbling water, the lowing of the herd.

His nostrils flared and he inhaled deeply. Inhaled the musty scent of buffalo. The scent of thick fur.

His stomach rumbled. Wolf instinct took over. He ran fast and hard into the clearing. The buffalo scattered. Ran.

But they were large beasts. Lumbering. Awkward.

Jamie raced after them. Swiftly. Gaining. Gaining on them.

He was so strong. So powerful. Much more powerful than an ordinary wolf.

A large buffalo stumbled to a stop and spun around to face Jamie. Jamie ground to a halt and brought his shoulders forward.

The buffalo snorted. Jamie saw the steam rise from its nose as it breathed in the cool night air. Jamie growled low in his throat and curled his lips back to bare his teeth.

The buffalo charged.

Jamie twisted and leapt to the side. The huge, hulking beast ran past him.

The buffalo spun around and released a loud, braying moo.

Jamie dropped his head back and howled—long and low. He snarled. Daring the animal to rush at him again.

The buffalo scraped the ground with a front hoof. Once. Twice. Then the other. Once. Twice.

Jamie crouched. His legs began to tremble, but not in fear. In anticipation.

The buffalo snorted. And then it charged.

Jamie tensed. Waited. His body drawn into a taut ball of muscle. Aching for release.

The buffalo ran toward him, its wide, craggy head bowed. Its massive shoulders a fur-covered mountain, blocking out the moonlight.

Jamie had never seen anything that looked so big—or so powerful. Jamie licked his chops. The buffalo rushed straight at him.

At the very last moment, Jamie sprang through the

air and sunk his large canine teeth into the throat of the buffalo. Its wounded cry echoed through the valley.

The buffalo staggered and stumbled to the ground.

Jamie sunk his teeth more deeply into its flesh. He tasted its blood.

Thick.

Hot.

Pumping into Jamie's mouth.

It tasted good.

Chapter
16

―――――――

Jamie growled low in his throat. He jerked his head to the side, ripping the buffalo's flesh wide open.

Blood spurted over him. Gushing like a river.

The animal bawled. It kicked. It jerked. Its eyes rolled back in its head. It fell to its side. Then it lay still. Dead.

Jamie tore at the muscle and flesh of the buffalo's throat. So good. Fresh. Fresh meat.

His feasted on his kill. Devouring the raw meat until his stomach was full. Then he licked the blood from his lips and paws. He curled up beside the massive beast he had killed and slept.

* * *

Jamie awoke. He squinted against the sunlight glaring into his eyes. His throat felt dry. Parched. He could smell the rusty scent of blood. And all around, he heard the insistent buzzing of flies.

He glanced down and gasped. Blood covered his body. Caked over his skin.

What happened? He shifted his gaze and saw the torn flesh of a buffalo. Flies darted around it. Jamie scrambled back and stared at the lifeless animal.

Memories of the night rushed through his mind.

His throat tightened. His stomach knotted. He gagged. I ate raw flesh from a living animal! I drank its blood! How could I do that? How could I?

He doubled over and rocked back and forth. Withering Woman turned me into a wolf.

His head throbbed. He thought—hoped—it was a dream. A nightmare brought on by the drink Withering Woman gave him. But it was real. He was a wolf.

Jamie stopped rocking. He looked at his hands. They were human hands. Human hands covered in dried blood. Strips of buffalo flesh and fur blackened his fingernails.

He jumped to his feet and ran to the river. He leapt into the water and swam to the center. He dunked himself over and over. He rubbed viciously at his skin.

So much blood! Everywhere. I can't get the blood off! I can't get it off. He scrubbed harder and harder until he realized that he was scratching and cutting himself, that the blood he saw belonged to him.

He waded back to shore, dragging his feet along the river bottom. What am I going to do?

He looked at the buffalo. If I hack off its head, no one would know how it died. I could claim that I killed it with my knife.

He walked into the forest. He cut off some tree branches and tied them together using the strips of leather fringe from his britches. He returned to the buffalo and severed its head.

With a great deal of effort, he shoved the carcass onto the litter he had made. He lifted the handles and began the long trek back to the village.

He arrived near nightfall. With long strides, he walked into the Shawnee camp and dumped the buffalo at Running Elk's feet. "Doubt me no more," he said.

The members of the tribe gathered around him. Touching him. Petting him as though he were a hero. He shouldered his way past them.

He saw Whispering Wind. She smiled shyly at him. His breath caught. Is she worth what happened to me last night?

He turned and stormed into Withering Woman's hut. She threw her head back and laughed when she saw him. "You had good hunting."

"What did you do to me?" he demanded.

"I made you mine!"

Jamie stared at the wrinkled crone. Her laughter echoed around him. "When the moon is full, you will change again. You will be my mate," she told him. "You will share the night with me."

"Never!" he cried, the rage burning through him. "I'll never again drink your poison."

"Once is enough," she said. "Once is all it takes."

"You must have the power to undo the spell," he yelled.

"Once it is done, it cannot be undone." She waved her hand in the air. "Each time the moon is full, you will turn into the wolf. For the rest of your days," she promised.

"And what about Whispering Wind?" he demanded. "Did you lie to me about that, too?"

"Go ask Whispering Wind to marry you. She will say yes."

Jamie dropped his gaze to the fire. She's lying. She must be lying. She tricked me once. Now she's trying to do it again. He spun on his heels and stalked out of the hut.

"Beware!" she called after him.

Jamie stopped and glanced over his shoulder.

Withering Woman wore a sinister smile. "Beware," she warned. "Beware. If ever your true love sees you while you are a wolf, you will remain a wolf forever."

Chapter
17

Jamie stomped out of the hut.

I don't believe her, he decided. I will not turn into a wolf again. She tricked me last night. But never again.

He heard soft footfalls coming toward him. He turned. Whispering Wind approached, her marriage blanket in her hands. She stopped and extended the blanket toward him.

She lowered her eyes. "I have fallen in love with you," she said softly. "I would have you as my husband if you will have me as your wife."

Jamie stared at the beautifully woven threads in the blanket. What would you think if I told you the truth? he wondered. Would you love me then?

He took the blanket from her. And in so doing, gave her his answer—he would marry her.

She took a step closer. "You must seal our pledge with a kiss," she told him quietly.

Jamie could not believe his ears. Withering Woman had given him power. He lowered his mouth to Whispering Wind's. She reached up and wrapped her arms around his neck, eagerly returning the kiss.

His heart filled with joy. But he couldn't stop his thoughts. Would you kiss me like this if you knew the truth? he wondered. Would you hold me close if you knew what I had become?

Whispering Wind stepped away from him. She slipped her fingers around the wolf tooth dangling from the leather strip around his neck. "Where did you get this?" she asked.

"Withering Woman gave it to me," Jamie told her. "She promised it would bring me luck." He smiled. "And it has."

Almost a month later, Jamie lay upon the floor of his bark-covered hut. He drew Whispering Wind's marriage blanket over him and his new wife. Whispering Wind snuggled against his side.

Chief Running Elk had married them that afternoon. He had glared at Jamie during the entire ceremony, but he was a true chief. He put his people before himself. And Jamie had found food for his people. They needed him.

Jamie could not believe it. You are mine, Whispering Wind, he thought with satisfaction. Mine. I traded my soul for you. You will remain mine forever! he vowed.

He gazed at his perfect wife. The moonlight crept through a hole in his roof and shimmered over her long black hair.

I love you, Whispering Wind. I love you so much. And you love me.

She had told him so often in the last month. She told him so every time he came back from a hunt.

He and the men had made many trips to the valley where Jamie discovered the buffalo. The village had plenty to eat now. He had won the respect of everyone in the tribe.

He avoided Withering Woman. He did not speak to her of the spell. He would never again drink her poison. He would never again become a wolf.

But she said once was all it took, Jamie thought. No, he told himself. She lied. I know she did.

He gazed at the stars through the hole in his roof. He smiled. Whispering Wind had made a wish before she had fallen asleep. A wish for a long and happy life together.

He was just closing his eyes when he saw the moon creeping over the hole in his roof. A bright orange orb in the black sky.

A full moon.

Jamie shivered with the cold. Then he grew hot. Unbearably hot. He threw off the blanket.

Whispering Wind stirred beside him. "What is it, my love?" she asked in a sleepy voice.

"Nothing," he told her. "I have to go outside. I need some fresh air." He sat up and tucked the blanket around her. "Sleep, Whispering Wind. I will return soon."

He slipped out of the hut and ran into the woods. Suddenly, the pain gripped him. Sharp. Deep. Racing through his entire body. He doubled over and dropped to his knees.

The tingling began. The tremors traveled through him.

"No!" he cried. "Nooo!" A long howl escaped his lips.

"Eyes of the Wolf! Where are you?" Whispering Wind called.

Withering Woman's warning echoed through Jamie's mind.

Beware. If ever your true love sees you while you are a wolf, you will remain a wolf forever.

I can't let her see me, Jamie realized. She loves me now. I'll stay a wolf forever!

He struggled to his feet and staggered to the bushes. He collapsed, his muscles quivering, his bones cracking.

"Eyes of the Wolf! Where are you? Come back to the hut," Whispering Wind called softly.

Jamie's heart thundered. If she sees me, I'm doomed! He heard her footsteps growing closer, closer.

He squinted through the darkness. He saw her silhouette in the moonlight. She walked toward him. "Eyes of the Wolf? Where are you?"

Jamie began to crawl on his stomach. His arms and legs were no longer those of a human. But the transformation was not complete. They were not yet the legs of a wolf.

He could not move fast. His muscles bunched and tightened. His jaw popped.

The bushes rustled. "Eyes of the Wolf, are you hiding in here?" Whispering Wind asked.

He saw her feet. He backed deep into the bushes. I can't let her see me. I can't let her see me.

His body jerked. The pain receded. The transformation was complete.

Jamie spun around, ready to flee. But there was nowhere to go.

A dead end! The side of a mountain loomed before him. He jumped up, trying to scale it. But his claws slid back down the smooth stone and he slammed into the ground.

He heard a startled cry. Growling low in his throat, he twisted around. And froze.

Whispering Wind stared straight at him!

Chapter
18

Jamie watched Whispering Wind's dark eyes grow round. The blood drained from her face.

With his keen eyesight, he could see her hands trembling. With his sharpened senses, he could smell her fear.

He could hear her heart. Pounding. Beating. Her blood thrumming through her veins.

Whispering Wind pointed to the tooth that still dangled from around his neck. "Eyes of the Wolf. You are Eyes of the Wolf! You are truly a wolf!" she cried. "I must tell Running Elk. I must warn the others!"

She ran. Back toward the village. Back toward

the warriors. Back toward those who would kill him.

I have to stop her. If the others learn the truth about me, if they learn what an unnatural creature I have become, they will kill me. I will not be safe anywhere. They will hunt me down. They will not give up until I am dead.

The instincts of the wolf took over. She was no longer Whispering Wind, the girl that he loved. The girl he had married. He saw her now only as the enemy.

She screamed now. Screamed for help. She would tell them. She would reveal his horrible truth to the others.

He rushed after her, his legs churning. Fast. Faster. Silently, darting into the shadows, into the moon-light.

His breathing came in harsh gasps. He raced toward the village. He saw Whispering Wind running through the trees. He saw her tiring. He could hear it in her breathing.

She stumbled and hit the ground. She gazed over her shoulder, her eyes wide. Wide with terror.

He growled. She staggered to her feet and began to run again.

But it was too late. He was too fast.

He sprang through the air. His front paws hit the center of her back. The force of his weight sent her to the ground.

She rolled over, flailing her arms. She struck his nose with her fists. His ears. His shoulders.

He bared his teeth. Saliva dripped from his mouth.

She released a long, high scream.

The last sound she made before he tore out her throat.

Chapter
19

Jamie awoke with the sunlight shining on his face. He lifted his hands. They were human hands. Joy and relief flooded his heart. He stared down at his body. Human again. He sighed with relief. With thankfulness.

The old woman lied to me, he realized. She lied. Whispering Wind saw me—and I did not remain a wolf forever.

He stood. The smell of blood assailed his nostrils. He spun around.

Whispering Wind!

She stared at him with lifeless eyes. He gazed down at her once lovely throat. Now it was a gaping hole. He pressed his hand to his mouth and stifled a moan.

Then he dropped to his knees and gathered her in his arms. He uttered a mournful cry.

Oh, Whispering Wind, I did love you. I did not want this to happen. But you gave me no choice. You would have told Running Elk. And he would have killed me.

Fighting down the bile rising in his throat, he stood and carried her body to the camp.

The women stopped their morning chores and rushed toward him. He tenderly laid Whispering Wind's body at the front of his home.

"She left our hut last night and was attacked by a wolf," he explained to them.

One woman nodded. She stepped toward him and rested her hand on his arm. "We will tend to her now. Go inside and rest."

Jamie nodded. Then he noticed Withering Woman standing at the opening of her hut. She caught his gaze. He saw her mouth curl in a cruel, knowing smile.

He turned away and stalked into his hut. He threw himself down on the blanket—the blanket he had shared with Whispering Wind. He fell into a deep sleep.

He woke up at nightfall. He rubbed his eyes and stepped outside his hut. The village stood silent. Whispering Wind's body was gone.

He saw Withering Woman sitting in front of her hut. She motioned for him to come to her. Jamie felt his body tense. He wanted to go back inside his hut.

Yet he felt her power, pulling him in her direction. Against his will, Jamie slowly moved toward Withering Woman.

She rose and slipped inside. He followed her. She spun around. Her eyes were black and glowing.

"You did not come to me last night," she scolded.

"I was too busy killing my wife!" he snarled. "You lied to me." He held out his hands. "She saw me, but I did not remain a wolf."

"Because hers was not a true love. It was a false love."

"Whispering Wind loved me," Jamie insisted.

"Loved you because of magic. That is not a true love," Withering Woman told him.

"You cannot hide from true love," she continued. "It will see through any disguise. Time cannot erode it. Pain cannot crush it. It marks the soul. Forever," Withering Woman said slowly. "Whispering Wind's was a false love, brought on by the spell I cast."

"The spell you cast," he repeated harshly. He took a menacing step toward her. "You turned me into an animal!"

"I gave you power!"

Power, he thought. Yes, she gave me power. Without another word, Jamie walked out of her hut. He ran silently, without leaving a trail. He ran fast and far.

He scrambled up the side of a mountain until he

came to a ledge. There he stopped to rest. Breathing heavily, he looked at the moon.

The moon.

A beautiful silver orb.

Now his enemy.

Behind the Iron Bars

My enemy! The moon was now my dreaded enemy.

He paced within the narrow confines. Six steps one way. Six steps back.

The memories followed his steps.

I left the Shawnee camp. Everything there reminded me of what I had done to Whispering Wind.

I lived in the woods. Whenever the moon was full, I suffered the pain of transformation. I grew into a wild animal.

I ate raw flesh. I greedily drank fresh blood.

I stalked and waited. I killed without mercy, without prejudice.

The small and meek.

The big and strong.

I wanted to blame Withering Woman, but I realized that she had wanted companionship, a friend, someone who shared her horrible secret.

I knew who was really to blame for all the misfortune and suffering in my life—Lucien Goode.

He tried to steal our food and water.

He killed my mother as surely as if he had pulled the trigger with his own hand.

He was the reason my poor father lost all reason—and met his gruesome death at the jaws of a wolf. He made everyone turn against us, desert us in the wilderness.

He convinced everyone that we were cursed.

I would never have been captured by the Shawnee if not for Lucien Goode.

I would never have met Withering Woman. Never have drunk her potion.

Never have become a wolf.

Now, I would have my revenge on Lucien Goode and his entire family. And all their descendants. I hated and despised them with every fiber of my being.

I lived only to take my revenge on them.

For three years, I searched for the Goodes.

During that time my hair turned silver—like the fur of a wolf. My eyes grew narrow.

It seemed that each time I transformed, a little

more of the wolf remained with me when the full moon passed.

Then one night when the moon rose high and full and I stalked the countryside, I took a deep breath. My nostrils flared.

I smelled the stench of Lucien Goode.

Chapter
20

The Settlement of
Crimson Falls,
1781

Jamie stood on the ridge and stared down at the Goodes' farm through silvery-blue eyes.

He felt the wind whip his shoulder-length hair around his face. I have found you, Lucien Goode, he thought, elated with victory. Now you and yours will pay the price for what I have become.

The farm stretched across acres of rich, fertile land. Jamie counted the large flocks of sheep, herds of fine horses and cattle. A vast red barn held rich stores of grain and hay.

The grand-looking farmhouse stood two stories high. Painted white with black shutters, it was surrounded by tall trees. A rich man's house if ever I've seen one, Jamie thought.

From the forest shadows, he watched Lucien Goode ride across the fields on his sleek brown horse, overseeing his many workers. He watched Lucien's daughters, Amanda and Laura, work in the garden behind the kitchen or sit sewing on the porch.

Jamie's lips curled in a smile of triumph. I will destroy you, Lucien Goode. I will acquire all that you hold precious. Your land, your stock, your fine house, and your carriage.

I will marry your daughter Laura. Pretty Laura who always thought she was too good for me. Then I will kill you. As Laura's husband, all your wealth will then belong to me.

After that I will no longer need Laura. I will destroy her—and Amanda.

I will not rest until your life, your family, and your fortune are in ashes.

Late that night, a full moon hung high in the sky. Jamie prowled through the woods—as a wolf.

Animals stilled when he passed. Silence reigned. The woods belonged to him.

For three months, Jamie had schemed and planned his revenge. He camped by the Goode farm . . . and waited. Waited patiently for the moon to rise—full and glowing. Each time it did, he gladly suffered through the transformation. When it was complete . . . he attacked.

The horses. The cows. The chickens.

Any animal that would be used to feed Lucien

Goode's fat belly. Any animal that would be used to bring gold coins to his pudgy hands.

Tonight his stomach felt full to overflowing with Lucien Goode's cow. Jamie had left other dead animals littered over the Goodes' land. Jamie's hated enemy would find them in the morning—just as he had found them in the past.

Jamie would watch from the cover of the trees. Just as he had in the past. Lucien's face would turn a mottled red. His eyes would bulge with anger. And he would yell—loud and long. Ordering his men to find and kill the wolf.

They would search high and low, but they would not find the wolf. They would never realize that it now walked among them—on two feet instead of four.

Jamie heard a twig snap. He froze, one paw in the air. He listened—with the ears of a wolf.

He sniffed the air. On the wind, he could smell the rancid odor of blood. The reminder of his night's work—the slaughter of Lucien Goode's livestock.

The beast within him hated the senseless slaughter of animals. But the man within him relished the taste of revenge.

Jamie heard a loud rustle. What was that? he wondered. He had fought a bear last month. A mountain lion the month before that.

What awaits me tonight? he wondered. What creature dares to invade my forest?

Then he caught the unmistakable stench.

Man.

He spotted balls of fire dancing through the trees. He heard voices.

"I found fresh tracks!" someone yelled behind him. "They must belong to that wolf that's been killing your livestock."

Jamie looked over his shoulder. He saw more balls of fire. Torches! he realized. Torches and men. And wherever men roamed, there were guns!

"Close the circle!" someone cried. "We'll get him tonight!" Jamie spun around. He could see the torches moving through the forest, closing in a circle. A circle around him.

I've been careless, he thought. Careless. He crouched low to the ground and began to run.

He felt something slither around his back foot. Suddenly, he was jerked through the air. He released a small cry.

He found himself hanging upside down. A length of rope tied to a branch held him prisoner, the rope's noose tightening around his paw.

A trap! I've been captured!

"Think we got him," a man yelled. "I heard a yelp."

The men's thudding footsteps grew louder. Closer.

Jamie's heart pounded hard in his chest.

Escape! I must escape!

He reached up and tried to wrap his front leg around the rope. He took a swipe at the rope. Missed.

He fell back down, dangling in the air. The torches moved faster through the woods. He could see them growing brighter, larger.

He heard the men thrash through the brush. They'll be here soon! he thought. Soon.

He took a deep breath and hurled his body upward. His front leg snagged the rope. He held it tightly and began to gnaw on the coarse rope, his sharp teeth serving as a saw.

Back and forth, back and forth. Sawing, sawing through the rope.

He heard the men's voices, growing louder. He gnawed faster. Faster.

The footsteps grew louder. Louder.

"Wait here!" a man yelled. "This is my land. The kill is mine."

Jamie's keen senses told him that one man had left the group. One man ran faster, harder. He could hear the man's heavy breathing. He heard the man's steps stop. "Got you!" the man cried.

Jamie lost his hold on the rope and fell back down, hanging in midair. A gun pointed straight at him.

He looked up at the man holding the gun. Looked up at Lucien Goode!

Jamie growled low in his throat. The stench of Lucien Goode filled his nostrils. He bared his teeth and snapped at the air.

Lucien Goode laughed. "Growl all you want. You're mine now. No one steals from me. No one! Not even a wolf." He aimed his rifle and fired.

Chapter
21

Jamie twisted in the air. He felt a burning pain in his shoulder. The bullet had grazed him.

He snarled and watched Lucien Goode drop to his knees and begin to reload his rifle. Jamie knew how long it could take to load a rifle. Especially in the dark.

Jamie struggled. His body swung back and forth. He leapt up and tried to grab the rope. He missed. He fell back down.

Snap!

The rope broke. His gnawing had weakened it. Jamie dropped to the ground.

Lucien Goode's eyes widened. The powder horn slipped from his hand. Gunpowder scattered over the ground.

Jamie took a step forward. He growled in the back of his throat and bared his teeth.

"Help!" Lucien yelled. "Someone help me!"

Jamie's nostrils filled with the scent of Lucien Goode. His mouth watered. He took another step forward, his lips curled back in a vicious snarl.

Lucien Goode stepped back, then stumbled and fell. "Oh, please. Someone help me!" he screamed.

Jamie crouched, ready to pounce upon his fallen prey.

Then his ears pricked up. His head snapped around. He heard the footsteps of many men. Close. Too close. He saw the flickering torches moving through the trees.

Lucien Goode cowered, crouched in a ball. Jamie heard him sob with fear. The sound made Jamie smile.

My revenge will have to wait. But we will meet again soon, Lucien Goode.

Then your tears will end, he silently promised. *Forever.*

He spun around and loped into the forest. He watched carefully for other traps. He heard his hunters' shouts. He heard rifles fire. A bullet whizzed past his ear. A lucky shot, he thought.

He heard the men call to each other to spread out. He looked over his shoulder and saw the torches burning in the distance. The hunters no longer formed a circle. He easily avoided them.

He began to run. Fast. Wild and free. He imagined

the taste of Lucien Goode's warm, red blood. The taste of his revenge.

A week later, Jamie walked through the woods—as a man. He saw a white sheet of paper nailed to a tree. It rustled in the breeze.

Cautiously, he approached. He read the words written in bold script on the white paper.

REWARD!

I will give five hundred dollars in gold to any man who brings me the head of the silver wolf.

Lucien Goode

Jamie laughed. Deeply. Long and hard. He snatched the bounty poster off the tree. Five hundred dollars! An incredible amount.

Is that what a dead wolf is worth to you, Lucien Goode? he wondered. Do you ever wonder why he attacks your livestock and no one else's?

You said my family was cursed. Now, the curse is on you.

The curse of the wolf.

Jamie strode through the woods. The time to make his move had arrived.

Chapter
22
___

Wearing his buckskin britches and jacket, Jamie stood on the porch of Lucien Goode's house. He knew he looked like a frontiersman. A man who knew his way around the Kentucky wilderness.

He knew he did not look like the young, frightened boy who had traveled along the Wilderness Road with his parents so long ago.

He was only twenty, but he looked much older. That was to his advantage. He did not want Lucien Goode to recognize him.

I will call myself Jack Snow, he thought. Jamie Fier is no more. Neither is Eyes of the Wolf. It is time for a new name. A new beginning.

He rapped his knuckles against the hardwood door. And waited. Waited to set his plan into motion.

The door opened. A young woman stood before him. Amanda Goode. He had seen her often from a distance. But never this close. She wore an apron over her fine blue dress. Her blond hair was swept up in a neat roll at the top of her head.

Jamie watched the pulse beat at her throat. Fast. It beat so fast. He imagined sinking his teeth—

"Jamie Fier!"

He snapped his gaze to her eyes. Her brown eyes. The color of mud. Only now they glowed with recognition.

Jamie stood there, speechless. How had she recognized him?

The woman laughed. "You probably don't remember me. Amanda. Amanda Goode."

"I remember you. I'm just surprised you recognized me." He swept his hat from his head. "I know I've changed—"

"Your eyes are the same," she said, smiling. "I always thought you had the most unusual eyes." She took his hand. "It's wonderful to see you. We were just getting ready to sit down to supper. Please join us."

Jamie forced himself to smile. I will have to alter my plans slightly, he realized, but she is taking me where I want to be. "I don't want to impose—"

"It's no imposition," she assured him, leading him into the house.

Once inside, Jamie inhaled deeply. He couldn't

remember the last time he'd been inside a house. He smelled food cooking and furniture polish. The air felt stuffy, smotheringly close.

He longed for the fresh air of the open fields and forests. But he must stay. It was necessary to his plan.

He could see stairs leading up to the next floor. To the bedrooms, he thought. Their bedrooms are probably up there.

He followed Amanda past a parlor on his right, an office on his left. She led him into the dining room. A fire burned brightly in the hearth. Amanda went to a cabinet and removed a plate. She set it on the table. "Please sit."

He took a seat and glanced around. "Will it just be you and me?"

"Oh, no. Papa should be here any moment. And my sister. I'm sure you remember her." Amanda walked to the doorway. "Laura! Supper is ready."

She looked at Jamie. "Laura felt a bit dizzy and needed to rest for a while. She hates it here. Especially since that horrid wolf has been attacking the livestock."

He heard light footsteps approach. Laura seemed to float into the room. Her blond hair flowed down her back. Her green eyes sparkled.

She is more beautiful than I remembered, he thought.

She wrinkled her nose and looked at him. "Who are you?"

"It's Jamie Fier," Amanda explained as she lifted a pot from the hearth and carried it to the table. "You remember him. His family traveled with us through the Cumberland Gap for a while."

Laura rolled her eyes. "Oh, yes. The cursed boy."

"We weren't cursed," Jamie said.

She waved her hand limply in the air. "Really, what does it matter?" She took a seat across from Jamie.

She has not changed, Jamie realized. She cares only for herself. Loves only herself. That will work very nicely with my plans. I cannot risk being around anyone who might love me truly.

A door on the far side of the room opened and Lucien Goode walked into the dining room.

Jamie's nostrils twitched. I would recognize his stench anywhere. He looks old and worried. Our meeting in the woods must have aged him. Good. Grow old, Lucien Goode. Grow old and weak before your time.

"Papa! Look who is here," Amanda said.

Lucien stared at Jamie. Jamie drew back his shoulders and raised his chin.

"It's Jamie Fier," she told him.

"Fier?" His eyes narrowed. "Figured you for dead."

"No, you only managed to kill off my mother and father," Jamie replied, unable to keep the anger from his voice.

"I'm not responsible for your father's death—or your mother's, for that matter," Lucien replied.

Stay calm, Jamie ordered himself. Stay calm. The day will come when you can unleash your anger and destroy him. But not yet. Savor the revenge. Make it sweet. As sweet as warm, flowing blood. Lucien Goode's blood.

"My apologies, Mr. Goode." Jamie forced himself to speak politely. "You are, of course, right. I was young. I found it easier to blame you than those I loved."

"How did your father die?" Amanda asked, true concern reflected in her eyes.

"A wild animal ripped out his throat," Jamie replied.

Laura gasped and covered her mouth. "I'm going to be sick. Must we discuss this before supper?"

"She's quite right," Mr. Goode agreed. "If you'll leave us now, young man—"

"I've already invited him to join us for supper, Papa," Amanda cut in.

"Stupid girl," her father snapped. "You should have checked with me first." He shook his head. "Never mind. We will share our food . . . even though you would not share yours, as I recall."

So he remembers, Jamie thought. Good. That will make my revenge that much sweeter.

Amanda ladled a large serving of stew into everyone's bowls and passed around a brown loaf of bread. Beneath his lashes, Jamie glanced at Laura. She will make a good wife, he thought. A wife who will never love me. Selfish and self-centered. Willful and full of complaints. As my wife she will finally know true unhappiness. True fear and pain.

"Tell us what happened after the wagonmaster abandoned you," Amanda prodded.

The wagonmaster? Your father abandoned me, Jamie thought. But he kept the anger from showing on his face. "I was captured by the Shawnee."

Amanda gasped and pressed her hand to her throat. "How dreadful! But you escaped."

Jamie ate a spoonful of his stew. "Eventually, but I learned a lot from them. I can move silently through the forest—like a shadow."

Lucien Goode snorted. "No one can move that quietly."

"I have become a skilled hunter." Jamie leaned back in his chair. "As a matter of fact, that's why I am here."

He reached into his shirt and pulled out the poster. Carefully, he unfolded it. "I saw this."

He eyed Lucien Goode suspiciously. "Five hundred dollars in gold is a great deal of money. You must be very wealthy, Mr. Goode."

"We're extremely rich," Laura boasted.

"Laura," her father scolded. "That's not fit talk for a young lady."

She shrugged. "I'm sure he knows, Papa. Everyone knows we're the wealthiest family in the valley."

"We have been most fortunate," Amanda added in a modest tone.

And soon you will be the most unfortunate, Jamie silently replied. He pushed his chair back from the table. "I can find this wolf for you," Jamie told Lucien Goode.

The older man laughed. "You? I've had the best trackers in the territory after that beast. Men who have been hunting those woods for thirty years and more."

"That may be true," Jamie began, "but I still say I can track him."

"I don't care what you say, boy," Lucien declared. "This wolf is—different. He outsmarts my men. We captured him a few nights ago and he escaped! He looked me in the eye like he knew me!"

Jamie folded the poster and slipped it back into his shirt. "I can find it. I can kill it."

"You're welcome to waste your time trying," Lucien replied.

"I need someone to show me where the wolf has been attacking. Perhaps your daughter—"

"Fine, fine," Lucien Goode mumbled. "Amanda has chores to do in the morning, but Laura is free. Laura, take him around tomorrow. Show him all he needs to know. I want this wolf's head hanging on my wall. I want his fur spread out into a rug in front of my fire so I can wipe my feet on him."

"There's just one thing," Jamie said.

Lucien Goode snapped his gaze from Laura to Jamie. "And that would be . . . ?"

"I don't want the money," Jamie explained.

Lucien Goode raised his eyebrows. "You'll do it for free?"

Jamie shook his head. "I want payment, but not your gold coins."

"Oh?" Lucien Goode stared at him, his eyes narrowed.

Jamie stared back with his silvery gaze. "I want to marry your daughter."

Lucien Goode chuckled. He splayed his fingers over his quivering belly. "I tell you what, Jamie Fier. Kill this wolf that has been causing me such grief and I'll give you anything you want. Meanwhile, I won't hold my breath."

Enjoy each breath you take, Jamie warned him silently. Sooner than you think, you'll be taking your last.

The next morning Jamie eagerly knocked on the Goodes' front door. A day with Laura, he thought smiling. Maybe I'll even steal a kiss or two. I might as well enjoy my time with her.

The door opened. Amanda stepped onto the porch holding a picnic basket. "Hello, Jamie," she said quickly. "I thought we might have a picnic after I show you around."

"Where's Laura?" he asked. "She was supposed to show me around."

"She's in bed with an awful headache. Her health is still very delicate. She often gets headaches and dizzy spells."

Jamie narrowed his eyes.

"Honestly," Amanda said as though she knew he did not believe her. Laughing lightly, she stepped off the porch. "Come on, Jamie. I'll show you around."

Jamie glanced up at the second-story windows. Soon, Laura, you won't be able to avoid me so easily, he thought.

He turned and watched Amanda swinging the picnic basket as she walked. He shook his head as he remembered the way she used to chase after him, telling him she loved him. She's grown up, he thought.

She made me welcome when I arrived, he thought. She treated me as a friend.

But she is a Goode. And she must die. They all must die.

With long strides, he caught up to her and took the basket from her hand. He looked at the land that stretched out before them. You would have been happy here, Mother, he thought. This land should have been ours. Very soon it will be.

In the distance he saw the cattle grazing near the woods. He heard them lowing. They could smell him just as he could smell them.

"The wolf usually attacks the cattle that are near the woods," Amanda told him.

"The trees offer him protection," Jamie replied.

She snapped her head around. "You really think you can catch him, don't you?"

Jamie shrugged. "He is hungry." *Hungry for power. Hungry for revenge.*

Amanda began to run. "Come on, Jamie! I want to show you something special."

He pretended that holding the picnic basket hampered his stride. He did not want her to see how fast he could run. He followed her into the woods.

She darted between the trees. In and out of the shadows. When he could not see her, he took a deep breath and captured her scent. And trailed after her.

Each time he transformed, more of his wolf skills and instincts stayed with him.

Soon Jamie heard the roaring sound of rushing water. The forest gave way to ridge. Just beyond it, Jamie saw the rushing waterfalls.

Amanda sat on the ground and motioned him over. He set the basket down and crouched down next to her.

"Isn't it beautiful?" she asked. "Sometimes you can see a rainbow in the falls." She reached into the basket and handed him a chicken leg. Jamie bit into the succulent meat. She had cooked it a little too much for the tastes he had acquired.

"Did you ever think of me over the years?" she asked.

"Yes," he answered honestly. "I thought of you, Laura, and your father." *I dreamed of the revenge I'd take on all of you,* he added to himself.

"I thought of you every day. I begged Papa to go back for you." Amanda sighed wearily. "But he wouldn't."

She placed her hand over his. "I always knew that someday you would belong to me. I never stopped loving you."

Chapter
23

⸻

Jamie froze. She can't love me! She can't. No one can love me. Not now. Not ever!

"I can't wait to marry you," she confided. "I know you'll find the wolf, Jamie. Soon, I hope."

Amanda thinks I want to marry her—not Laura.

He remembered Amanda begging him to marry her so he wouldn't be left alone on the trail. He remembered her always grabbing his hand, saying she loved him.

But that was years ago. She was just a kid. She can't really love me. Can she?

Jamie's throat tightened. I cannot let her love me. It is too dangerous. I would become a wolf forever if she saw me while I was transformed.

When she finds out I intend to marry Laura, she will hate me. I'll be safe then, Jamie thought.

"Jamie, what's wrong?" she asked.

Jamie swallowed hard. Yes, I must make Amanda hate me. I will encourage her feelings. Lead her on. I'll let her think she's the one I want to marry until I bring Lucien a wolf. Then I will choose Laura—and break Amanda's heart.

That will be fitting revenge for Amanda. She will surely hate me then. And I will be safe.

He raised his silvery gaze to her own. "I had forgotten how pretty you were," he lied.

She blushed. "Oh, Jamie," she whispered. "I've waited so long for you to say something like that. To notice me. To truly notice me."

He leaned toward her. Close. Closer. He pressed his lips to hers. Eagerly she returned his kiss.

Jamie pulled away. He began to feel a little bad about what he was doing to Amanda. She is a Goode, he reminded himself again. She is your enemy. And she is dangerous to you.

Amanda rose to her feet. "Stand at the edge with me." She walked to the edge of the cliff.

How easy it would be to slip quietly behind her— and push. Her scream would echo over the falls.

I should do it, he thought wildly, still disturbed by her confession of love. I should kill her now and rid myself of her threat.

He came to his feet. He still wore moccasins. They cushioned his steps, made him silent. He stepped toward her, lightly, cautiously.

A hard push. A gentle push. She stood so close to the edge that either would work. But that would cheat him.

Because of her family he had lost both his parents. Because of her family, he'd been left behind in the mountains.

None had spoken up for him. Not even Amanda, who had professed her love.

Because of her family's greed, he had been captured by the Shawnee. Because of her family, he suffered through the transformation at each full moon and became a wolf.

It was only right that the wolf should kill them. Should slaughter them all.

She tilted her face back and closed her eyes. "Can you feel the mist?" she asked.

The falls roared. The water gushed over the high rocks and pounded into the river below.

"Crimson Falls," she whispered reverently. "Do you know why they call it that?"

"No."

She turned and smiled. "I love the story. Once an Indian warrior loved an Indian maiden. But he thought she didn't love him. He wanted her love so desperately that he gave his soul over to the wolf during a full moon in exchange for her hand in marriage."

A shiver crept along Jamie's spine. The story was too close to the truth. He did not want to hear the rest, but he could not stop himself from asking, "What happened?"

"One night, when the moon was full, he crept from their hut and turned into a wolf. The maiden followed him. When she saw that he was a wolf, her heart broke. She threw herself into the falls. And died."

Foreboding swept through Jamie. "What happened to the warrior?"

"He leapt into the falls as well," she told him. "The legend says that for a month, the falls flowed red in sorrow. So they called the settlement Crimson Falls."

"A silly story," Jamie said. He turned on his heel, wanting to believe that it was only a story—and not the truth.

"Do you know why he jumped?" she called after him.

Jamie spun around. The smile had left her face and her dark eyes glowed. She took a step toward him. "He learned too late that she truly loved him. And the legend says that when she looked at him, he knew he would remain a wolf forever."

"Legend," he said. But he knew legends were rooted in truth.

Amanda reached out and wrapped her hand around the tooth that dangled from a leather strip at his neck. "What a strange necklace," she said. "They say the Indian warrior wore a wolf's tooth around his neck."

Jamie stiffened. How does she know all this? he wondered. "This was a gift of the Shawnee. It doesn't mean anything," he lied. "Your story is just a legend," he repeated, growing irritated.

"I suppose you're right," she said. "Our servant

knew so many Indian legends, and she could tell them so well. She almost made me believe them all."

Jamie furrowed his brow. "What servant?"

She grabbed his hand, and started walking. "Don't you remember? I told you we had an Indian servant when we were growing up."

He remembered now. Remembered her prattling about Indians and her servant.

"She told me that wolves have keener senses," Amanda continued. "They can see in the dark. She knew so much about them that sometimes I imagined she really was a wolf."

Jamie stumbled to a stop and jerked his hand free of her grasp. She spun around and stared at him. "What? What's wrong now?" she asked.

"What happened to your servant?" he asked, dreading the answer.

"She was incredibly unhappy. Her mother was Shawnee, and her father was a French fur trader. People were suspicious of her because of her Indian blood, so she returned to the Shawnee."

Jamie's heart felt as though it had turned into a block of ice. "Have you seen her since you moved to Kentucky?" he asked.

Amanda shook her head. "No, but I'd like to see her. I'd know her anywhere. She looked so unusual."

"In what way?" Jamie asked, afraid he already knew the answer, but needing to hear Amanda say it. To confirm his suspicions.

"It's hard to describe. She was only about ten years

older than I was, but she looked like—" Amanda furrowed her brow. "She looked like an old woman, all wrinkled and bent. With white streaks in her hair."

She smiled brightly. "That's why the Indians called her Withering Woman."

Chapter
24

Withering Woman!

Jamie felt the blood drain from his face. What else? Had she ever confessed that during a full moon, Withering Woman, herself, turned into a wolf?

"Jamie! Jamie!"

He heard Amanda's voice from far away. The waterfalls thundered through his head. The world swirled around him. Mountains. Trees. Falls. Amanda.

Wide brown eyes, staring at him. Watching him.

Why does she stare at me like that? So intensely? Can she see the truth about me?

Does she know what I will become when the moon grows full? Is that why she keeps talking about wolves and warriors who turn into wolves?

Jamie walked back to the ledge and stared out. He feared the legend of Crimson Falls was no legend at all. Had Withering Woman cast her spell before? Had others traded their souls for love?

Was Withering Woman as young as Amanda claimed she was? Or was she as old as Jamie believed—as ancient as the mountains and the wind?

"Jamie?"

He felt Amanda's soft fingers curl around his arm. "Jamie? What's wrong? You look so pale. You look ill," she said, genuine concern in her voice.

"Who told you the story of Crimson Falls?" he asked hoarsely.

"Withering Woman. She made the place sound beautiful. That's why Papa wanted to move here. I think it is beautiful."

"What else did she tell you?"

She sighed. "She taught me some secrets of healing. Just a few things here and there. Why?"

Jamie spun around. His blood felt chilled to the bone. "No reason."

He looked deeply into Amanda's eyes. He saw innocence. She knows only the legend, he decided. Not the truth.

"We need to get back," Jamie told her. "It'll be dark soon. I'd hate to think what would happen if the wolf found you out alone at night."

"So what do you think?" Lucien Goode asked. He stuffed tobacco into his pipe. "Do you think you can kill this thieving wolf?"

"Yes, sir," Jamie replied, full of confidence. "I think he lives in the mountains and only comes down because he is hungry." Hungry for revenge, Jamie thought.

Jamie had enjoyed the evening meal, sharing it with the Goodes. He forced himself to return Amanda's warm glances. But his gaze kept returning to Laura.

Laura sat with them in the parlor now, her needle-point in her lap. Her fingers moved sluggishly over the handiwork as though she really had no interest in it.

Perhaps I shall wait a while before I kill you, Laura, he thought to himself. I could enjoy your company in the evenings. He turned his face toward the fire burning low in the hearth. He did not want anyone to see his smirk.

Perhaps I won't kill you at all. You are no threat to me. Since you do not love me, your eyes can see me as a wolf—and no harm will come to me. You could keep me company through the years.

Your punishment will be to be treated with the same cold disdain and cruelty you've always shown me. You will come to curse the day we married.

And you will remain my wife—in my power—forever.

And what of Amanda? Perhaps I will not kill her either. Her punishment will be rejection and pain when she learns I will not marry her. Pain and loneliness as deep as the love she professes to feel for me.

A lifetime of heartache and sadness will be my revenge upon her.

But Lucien. Lucien must die—exactly as my father did. The thought filled him with anticipation.

"Those dishes took forever to clean!" Amanda exclaimed as she hurried into the room. She sighed. "I thought I'd never finish."

Jamie turned from the fire. Amanda looked at him with love in her eyes. He wouldn't feel safe until he saw her eyes filled with pain and hatred.

Soon. Soon that would happen.

"Did you show Jamie where we nearly captured the wolf?" her father asked.

"No, Papa. I didn't think I needed to. I showed him Crimson Falls instead." She looked slyly at Jamie and lowered her voice. "And I learned his secret."

Chapter
25

Jamie's heart pounded so loudly that he could hear it. His mouth grew dry.

My secret! She knows the truth about me!

Laura scooted forward in her chair. "I love secrets. Tell us," she urged excitedly. "Tell us Jamie's secret."

No, Jamie thought. Don't tell them. He found it difficult to breathe. He wanted to run. Like a wolf. Run swiftly to safety.

"Come on, girl," Lucien demanded. "Tell us."

Amanda bit on her lower lip and looked at Jamie. She smiled secretively. "He thinks legends are silly."

Jamie released a shaky breath. His true secret remained safe.

Laura plopped back in her chair. "You didn't tell

him that silly story about how Crimson Falls got its name, did you?"

"I think it's romantic," Amanda told her.

"What's romantic about two people jumping off a cliff and killing themselves?" Laura asked. "And someone turning into a wolf. Who would believe that could happen?"

"I didn't say I believed the story," Amanda said. "I simply find it interesting."

Jamie breathed a sigh of relief. He was right. Amanda didn't believe the legend. She didn't know the truth.

"It was an interesting story, but I agree with Laura. Totally unbelievable," Jamie said.

Laura looked at Jamie. "I never thought you and I would agree on something."

Jamie smiled at her. "You never know what people think."

Laura returned to her needlework. After a moment, she dropped her head back and rubbed her eyes. "I'm beginning to think I need spectacles," she said. "The needle keeps blurring and I can't see what I'm doing."

"Maybe you're just tired," Amanda said, concern in her voice.

Laura pressed the back of her hand to her forehead in a dramatic gesture. "I think you're right. I'm going to bed." She set the needlework aside and rose to her feet. She swayed.

Amanda rushed over and slipped her arm around Laura. "What's wrong?" Amanda asked.

Laura shook her head. "I'm just dizzy. Will you fix me some warm milk?"

Jamie almost exploded with laughter. Laura was such an actress, pretending to be in ill health so she'd be treated like a princess.

Laura was fine before Amanda walked into the room, he thought. And fine during the meal. Now Amanda is waiting on her like a servant.

Well, all that will change once we are married, he decided. Soon everything will change.

A few nights later, Jamie stalked through the mountains, clutching the long rifle. He had seen a den of wolves near the base of the mountain.

He had grown to despise the way man hunted. He saw no sport in it. Using a long rifle and killing from a hiding place did not give him the opportunity to gaze into his prey's eyes. Smell its fear. Match wits and power. Truly battle for life.

But tonight, he could not take any chances. The time had come to put the final steps of his plan into action. When he located the empty cave, he crouched behind a bush and waited, his long rifle aimed at the opening in the rocks.

Near dawn he heard the low howls and the teasing barks. He saw the large, silver male wolf approach.

The wolf he wanted.

The wolf's brown mate and three cubs followed it to the cave. A family. A family Jamie would destroy.

The wolves suddenly stopped. The silver wolf sniffed the air.

He smells me, Jamie realized. He aimed his rifle and pulled the trigger.

Nothing happened.

The wolf growled and lunged into the thicket where Jamie hid. It knocked Jamie to the ground.

Jamie stared up into a mouthful of keen-edged teeth. Saliva dripped on him from the wolf's open jaws. He felt the animal's full weight pressing down on his chest. Squeezing out his breath. Pinning him to the ground.

Jamie knotted his hands in the thick fur at the beast's throat. He pushed back with all his strength.

The wolf snapped its massive jaws in Jamie's face. Jamie felt the animal's hot breath on his skin.

Jamie shoved at the ground with his foot. He sent them rolling down the side of the hill. Over and over until they landed near the bottom.

The wolf bounced off Jamie. Jamie reached for his beaded sheath and pulled out a large knife. He scrambled to his feet.

The wolf snarled and crouched down. Jamie knew the wolf's mind, knew how to think like a wolf. He waited.

The wolf barked and sprang into the air. It landed on Jamie and, again, knocked him to the ground.

Jamie pushed back the wolf's head with his arm. Then plunged his knife into its heart.

The silver beast howled and grew still. Jamie shoved the dead animal off his chest. He stared at the wolf.

"Lucien Goode is responsible for your death," he said quietly. "My revenge will be yours as well."

He hefted the wolf onto his back and pulled its legs over his shoulders. Then he strode back to the Goode farm with his prize—the wolf he had tracked and killed.

You're not the wolf that has been attacking Lucien Goode's livestock, Jamie acknowledged with a satisfied grin. No, that wolf captured you.

He was surprised how often he thought of himself as a wolf. With each passing full moon, his senses grew sharper. He heard beetles scurrying through rotting logs. Squirrels snoring in trees while they napped.

The Goodes' house came into view. Jamie shifted the weight across his broad shoulders. He inhaled deeply, then smiled. Yes, he would find Lucien Goode at home.

He crossed the yard. Carefully balancing the wolf, he knocked loudly on the door.

Lucien appeared. Jamie dropped the dead wolf at his feet. "I've come to claim my reward," he announced.

Lucien's eyes widened. "That's the wolf that's been killing my livestock! I'd recognize him anywhere." He crouched down and examined the animal. "How did you kill him?"

"With my knife," Jamie explained. "He attacked me. I had no choice."

Lucien glanced up. His eyes narrowed. "You have

impressed me, Jamie Fier. I never expected that." He stood. "Come to my study and we will discuss the particulars of your reward." Jamie followed Lucien into the house.

"Amanda! Laura!" Lucien yelled. The girls scurried out of the kitchen. "Jamie killed the wolf and now he wants his reward. Come into my office, all of you."

Jamie followed Lucien into his study. Lucien took his seat behind a large wooden desk. Jamie stood in front of it, Amanda and Laura beside him.

Amanda flung her arms around his neck. "Oh, Jamie, I'm so glad you finally killed the wolf. We can get married now. Isn't it wonderful?" she gushed.

Jamie grabbed her wrists and pulled her away. "I don't want to marry *you*. I want Laura."

Amanda's face turned deathly pale. Tears welled in her dark eyes.

Jamie saw all he had hoped for. Pain. Grief. Rejection.

"You don't mean that," Amanda sobbed. She clung to Jamie's arm. "She doesn't love you. She'll never love you like I do."

"But she is the one I want to marry." Jamie coldly pushed her away.

He turned his attention back to Lucien Goode. "Will you give me your blessing to marry Laura?"

"Oh, my!" Laura cried out. She pressed the back of her hand to her forehead. "I think I'm going to swoon." She gracefully crumpled to the floor.

Lucien got up from his chair and hurried to her side. Grunting and groaning, he lifted her into his arms. He glanced over his shoulder at Jamie. "I'm getting too old for this. She needs a husband who can carry her to her room every time she faints. You have my blessing."

Victory surged through Jamie while he watched Lucien carry Laura from the room. I can smell it in the air. Revenge is hovering nearby, and it is so sweet. So incredibly sweet.

Amanda stepped toward him and slapped his face. His cheek stung, but the anger in her eyes pleased him.

"You made me think you wanted to marry me," she cried. "I hate you, Jamie Fier. I hate you with all my heart. You will regret not marrying me."

Chapter
26

Amanda hated him. Jamie held back his smile of satisfaction. Her words filled him with relief.

He watched her run from the room, tears streaming down her face. A small part of Jamie regretted that he had hurt her. But her love had left him no choice.

You should hate your father for this as well, Amanda, he thought. He destroyed my family. And now I am destroying his.

The following day, Jamie and the Goodes traveled to the heart of the settlement for the marriage ceremony.

At breakfast, Laura claimed she didn't feel well

enough for the long ride into town. But Jamie had insisted.

For once, Lucien Goode had agreed with him.

As the wagon rolled through the countryside, Jamie sat in the back with Amanda. Lucien Goode and Laura sat on the bench seat.

Jamie glanced over to find Amanda glaring at him, her arms crossed over her chest. The same way she'd been looking at him all morning.

Her anger amused him. She hadn't spoken a single word to him since the night before. Laura hadn't stopped complaining.

My head hurts.

I feel faint.

I think I might bring up my meal.

Jamie smiled. Her attempts to stop the marriage were futile.

"I suppose you'll enjoy playing nursemaid to your sickly wife," Amanda said finally.

"She is beautiful. She will make me very happy," Jamie answered.

"She won't cook for you or wash your clothes or care for you." Amanda leaned forward, her eyes glassy and hard. "She'll never care for you like I would have, Jamie."

"I told you long ago, when we were traveling through the Cumberland Gap, that I would never marry you," he reminded her.

"You still hate us, don't you?" she whispered harshly. "You're trying to punish me because of what Papa did."

He averted his face to hide the hatred boiling in his eyes. Yes! I hate you. And Laura. And your father.

If you only knew—if you only knew everything that your father has done to me.

Soon. Soon you will know. Soon all of you will know.

"I hate you!" she spat.

I'm glad, he thought. He wanted to hear those words again and again. The words that would keep him safe from the final curse of the wolf.

The wagon rolled through the huge front gates of the fort that served as the capital of the Crimson Falls settlement. Many of the farmers, like Lucien Goode, lived in outlying areas. Some people preferred to live closer to the fort, their houses built within its wall.

Jamie had never been inside a fort. It was a huge rectangular structure. Cabins lined its walls, their back sides providing extra protection against Indian attacks.

The roofs only sloped in one direction—away from the back walls. Although it looked odd, Jamie could see the wisdom in that design. Men could lie on top of the roofs with some protection and shoot the enemy.

Three additional log cabins stood in the center of the fort. The gunsmith shop. A jail. A meeting hall.

Lucien brought the wagon to a halt in front of the meeting hall. Jamie hopped out of the back of the wagon. He helped Laura down.

Once her feet touched the ground, she slumped against him, pressing her cheek to his shoulder. "Oh,

Jamie, do we have to do this today? I feel so dizzy. So weak. I can barely stand."

He cupped her chin and tilted her face back. He was surprised to see that she had grown incredibly pale. Sweat beaded her brow and upper lip.

"It's just nerves, Laura," Jamie said curtly. "You'll feel better once we're married."

She shook her head slightly. "I think I'll feel worse."

Jamie grasped her arm and led her into the meeting hall where the minister waited. He held Laura snugly against his side, supporting her while the minister performed the ceremony.

Jamie could feel tiny shivers racing through Laura's body. She's talented, Jamie thought. She would have gone far on the stage. She should have pursued it.

The minister cleared his throat. "Does anyone know a reason why these two should not wed?"

Jamie looked over Laura's head and stared at Amanda. He could see her chin begin to quiver. She parted her lips. Then her gaze met Jamie's. She pressed her lips together into a straight line.

"Very well," the minister said. "Do you, Laura Goode, take Jamie Fier to be your husband?"

"I do," she whispered.

"And do you, Jamie Fier, take Laura Goode to be your wife?"

"I do," he boomed.

"Then I now pronounce you man and wife."

Laura fell into a crumpled heap on the floor.

Jamie crouched beside Laura and patted her cheek. "Laura? Laura, wake up."

Her eyelids fluttered. She sighed. "I don't feel good."

Amanda knelt beside her and took her hand. "It's all the excitement of being a bride," Amanda told her sister.

"I don't feel very excited," Laura said. "I just feel tired."

Amanda glared at Jamie as though to say, "I told you so."

Jamie slipped his arms around Laura and lifted her from the floor. Lucien wiped his brow. "She's always fainting. Glad she has you to carry her now."

Jamie carried Laura out to the wagon and settled her in the back. They began the long trek back to the Goodes' homestead.

By the time the wagon rolled to a stop in front of the house, it was already dark. Jamie jumped out of the back. "Come on, Laura," he said impatiently. He pulled her up roughly by the arm.

She would soon learn that her fake illness would do her no good.

"Oh, Jamie," she mumbled. "I feel sick."

"Fine, then," he said. He pulled her toward him. Then lifted her into his arms. Her head lolled against his shoulder.

"Amanda," she called weakly. "Amanda?"

Amanda climbed down from the wagon and took her sister's hand. "What is it, Laura?"

"I feel so dizzy. Could you please fix me some warm

milk and bring it to my bedroom? I always sleep so much better after I drink your warm milk."

"Of course," Amanda said. She walked away without looking at Jamie.

Jamie had expected her to object to the marriage during the ceremony. He wondered why she hadn't. Maybe Amanda decided that having Laura as a wife will be punishment enough, he thought.

Jamie trudged into the house carrying Laura's limp body. She felt heavier and heavier as he climbed the stairs.

"Last bedroom on the right," Laura said in a soft voice. Jamie stalked down the hallway and walked into her room—their room.

You are my wife now, Laura. But how little you know of the man you married. How fitting that our wedding night will be blessed with a full moon.

He laid her on the bed. The wooden slats that supported the mattress squeaked. Laura draped her hand over her brow. "I'm so sorry, Jamie. I'm sorry I fainted when we finished exchanging our vows."

He knelt beside the bed and patted her hand. "It's all right, Laura. We're still married. Now nothing can change that."

She began to breathe in short, shallow pants. Her fingers tore at the white collar of her dress. "I can't breathe." She gasped. "I need air. I must have air. Please . . . please open the window."

"Certainly, Laura." He stood and walked to the window. He jerked the curtains aside. He looked at the night sky. The moon would soon rise.

He heard soft footfalls and turned. Amanda stood in the shadowed doorway, lit by the candle she held. He looked into her eyes. Black pools. Unfathomable. Jamie couldn't tell what she felt, what she thought.

She held a glass of milk in her free hand. She walked into the room and set the candle on the bedside table. The flame flickered. Ignoring Jamie, she sat on the bed and slipped her hand beneath Laura's head. Laura moaned.

"Come on, Laura, you need to drink this," Amanda urged in a soft but firm voice.

Jamie watched while Laura wrapped her hand around the glass and brought it to her lips.

"I'm going to talk to your father," Jamie said. He began to walk across the room. "Can you stay with Laura for a while?"

Amanda nodded and looked over her shoulder. "I'd do anything for you, Jamie. Anything. I love you. I know I shouldn't. I know I should hate you. But I can't. I still love you."

Chapter
27

Jamie stumbled to a stop and spun around. "You don't mean that," he snapped. He could feel his pulse pound. Blood rushed in his ears.

"I know I said I hate you. I wanted to. But I guess I'll always love you, no matter what you do," she confessed.

"I wish you and Laura every happiness," she added quietly. She turned her attention back to her sister. Jamie stepped into the hallway. His legs felt weak.

She loves me! This changes all my plans. Now I will have to kill her. She has left me with no choice.

But first he had to take care of her father. Jamie rushed down the stairs and barged into Lucien

Goode's study. Lucien sat in a chair beside the fire, smoking a pipe and reading a newspaper. He glanced up.

"Mmm. I suppose you'll be living here now," he said without emotion.

"Yes, sir, I suppose I will," Jamie said, breathing heavily. Jamie walked to the window. "Do you mind if I pull the curtains back?"

Lucien waved his hand in the air. "Make yourself at home."

Oh, I will, Jamie thought. I will definitely make myself at home. Jamie pulled the curtains aside, stared into the black night . . . and waited.

Waited for the full moon to rise high in the night sky. He could see the wind growing stronger, bending the limbs of the trees. It will be a good night, he thought, a good night to take my revenge.

He could see the shafts of moonlight piercing the night shadows. He dropped his head back and waited.

"Papa?"

Jamie spun around at the sound of Amanda's voice. She stood in the doorway.

"Papa, I thought I'd go for a walk. Now that the wolf has been killed, it should be safe," she said.

Lucien pointed to a rifle hanging above the hearth. "Load the rifle and take it with you. Just in case."

Amanda strolled across the room. Hurry! Jamie thought. Hurry. He saw the full moon, climbing to its summit. Almost there. Only a moment away . . .

He couldn't allow Amanda to see him as a wolf. It would destroy him.

Amanda took the rifle from the rack and walked to her father's desk. She uncapped the powder horn and tilted it toward the barrel of the rifle. Powder scattered over her father's desk. She sighed. "I've never been very good at this."

Jamie rushed across the room. "Here. I'll do it for you." He grabbed the horn and poured powder down the barrel.

"Not too much there, Jamie," Lucien remarked. "I don't want the gun to explode in her face."

Jamie dropped the powder horn. He wrapped the tiny cloth around the lead ball and slipped it into his mouth. His hands trembled. His mouth felt dry.

Relax, he commanded himself. You have time. His mouth began to fill with saliva. He rolled the cloth and ball in his mouth. He removed them, dropped them into the barrel, and jammed them into place with the rod. Then he added the additional powder.

He handed the rifle to Amanda. "There."

She looked at him, her eyes warm. "Thank you, Jamie. Laura fell asleep so I thought it was safe to leave her."

"You should get started on your walk. It's getting late," he said, anxious to get her out of the house.

"Do you want to come with me?" she asked.

"No!"

Her eyes grew wide. Jamie took a breath to calm himself. "No, I want to speak with your father."

Amanda pressed a kiss to her father's cheek. "'Night, Papa. I'll probably be a while, so don't wait up for me."

He grunted and returned to reading his newspaper. Amanda strolled out of the room. Jamie crossed back over to the window. He stared up at the night sky. He didn't have to see the moon to become a wolf. But he liked knowing when the transformation would begin.

He saw the silver globe rising in the sky. Clouds passed before it. Its light spilled through the shimmering wisps.

He felt the tingling in his limbs begin. Jamie could hear his harsh breathing echoing around him. He felt the first tremors in his body.

And then the pain—sharp like a knife through his heart.

Tonight, finally, the pain will be worth it. The agony of transformation will give me what I want most— revenge!

He doubled over and fell to his knees.

Lucien Goode came up out of his chair. "What's wrong with you? Are you sick, too?" he asked, alarm in his voice.

Jamie snapped his head up and glared at his enemy. "Watch me, Lucien Goode," he snarled. "Watch me and see what your betrayal cost me."

"What . . . what are you talking about?" Lucien asked.

Jamie growled low in his throat and bared his teeth. He knew his silver eyes held a wild glow. He could feel it. The untamed power coursed through him like a raging river.

"What's happening to you?" Lucien Goode demanded. "What are you doing?"

Lucien backed up a step. Then another. "What's going on?" he asked.

Jamie heard the panic in his voice. He smelled the sweat on the older man's flesh.

Soon. Very soon. He'd taste the blood of Lucien Goode . . .

Jamie closed his eyes and allowed the agony of the transformation to consume him. When the torment passed, he opened his eyes and looked at Lucien Goode with the eyes of a wolf.

Lucien Goode backed up against his desk. His eyes bulged from their fatty sockets. His pipe fell from his limp hand. "Withering Woman . . . she told us stories. Legends. I had no idea she spoke the truth! I never would have believed it if I hadn't seen it with my own eyes," Lucien gasped.

Lucien's gaze darted around the room. Jamie crouched and snarled.

Find a weapon, Lucien Goode, he dared. Attack me. Prolong your death.

A smell assailed his nostrils. Rancid and sweet at the same time. Fear! I can smell fear.

His stomach grumbled. His mouth began to salivate. His heart pounded. I can smell your fear, Lucien. I can see it. I can hear your harsh breathing.

Lucien scrambled across the room toward the fireplace. He grabbed a poker and pointed it at Jamie. "I should have known. You said you were captured by the Shawnee. Things are beginning to make sense now. You're the wolf! You're the wolf that killed my livestock. Everything else was a trick."

Lucien swung the poker in an arc. His eyes glittered. "It's a shame you didn't die with your parents. But you will die tonight!"

Lucien lunged for Jamie. The tip of the poker scraped Jamie's snout before he leapt away. Jamie rolled out his tongue. Blood dripped onto it. His blood.

He crouched low. Lucien stood in front of the window. He jabbed the poker in the air.

Their eyes met and held. Enemies. Hated enemies.

Jamie curled back his lips and licked his chops. He snapped his jaws, his sharp teeth hitting each other. *Clack! Clack!*

He raised his back and hunched his shoulders. He growled deep within his throat. His powerful muscles grew taut. Then released.

He leapt into the air. Jaws open. His gaze fixed on the pale throat of Lucien Goode.

Lucien flung the poker at Jamie with all his strength. Jamie saw it hurtling through the air. A sharp, iron spear. Flying straight at his heart.

Chapter
28

———

Jamie twisted in the air. The poker grazed his side and clattered to the floor.

Jamie's front paws struck Lucien's chest and sent him staggering backward. His heavy body crashed through the glass window.

Jamie felt his body carried through the window on top of Lucien. Shards of glass sprayed over Jamie. He squeezed his eyes shut.

Lucien landed with a thud. Jamie straddled his chest. He pushed his face close to Lucien's. He curled back his lips and bared his long, sharp fangs. Lucien's eyes widened.

"Nooo!" Lucien cried. He fought to push Jamie off. He pounded Jamie's chest.

But Lucien's weak, flabby arms were no match for Jamie's strength. Lucien was like a turtle turned over on its back—helpless.

Lucien stopped struggling. His eyes filled with dread. Filled with knowledge.

"No!" he screamed again. "I know you blame me, but your mother's death was an accident. We had no choice but to leave you and your father. We'd seen the Shawnee. We knew they were near. We couldn't wait for you to fix your wagon! It would have endangered us all."

You knew! You knew you were sentencing us to death. Now, I sentence you! Jamie thought victoriously.

Jamie growled low in his throat. A growl of victory. Utter satisfaction.

Then he sunk his teeth into Lucien's soft throat. He savored the taste.

Lucien screamed shrilly. Then choked as blood gurgled from his mouth.

His body jerked and twitched. Then it grew completely still. Lifeless.

Jamie watched as his enemy's eyes glazed over. He lifted his head back and howled—long and low.

A lonesome sound. The cry of a wolf.

Jamie had little time to savor his revenge. He glanced around the yard behind the house. What if Amanda had heard the shattering glass? What if she had heard her father scream? What if she ran to help him?

It only takes one look—one look to seal my fate.
Snap!

Jamie heard a twig break. He jerked his head up and stared into the darkness. Was Amanda near?

He needed to hide from Amanda's eyes. Eyes filled with love.

Slowly he backed up, one paw behind another. He would be safe in Laura's room. She does not love me, he thought. I can hide there until morning. Then I'll deal with Amanda.

He took one last look at Lucien Goode sprawled in a pool of his own glistening blood.

Then he leapt through the broken window, back into the study. Slowly, cautiously, Jamie stalked out of the room and up the stairs. At the top, the hallway was dark. Shadowed.

He stopped and listened. A hushed silence filled the house. He could hear the crickets outside. The hooting of an owl. But inside, he could hear nothing but eerie quiet.

As though someone—or something—waited.

You're imagining things, he told himself. Amanda is out walking. Laura is asleep. Lucien Goode is dead.

He saw a pale light at the end of the hallway, spilling out of Laura's bedroom. He neared the bedroom. He breathed deeply. The smell of blood remained strong on his fur, but beyond it, he could smell Laura.

Lavender. She always smelled of lavender. And he could smell the lingering scent of fear.

Did she hear her father's cry? Is she inside, hiding, afraid? Will I be forced to kill her, too?

He crept to the partially opened door. He nudged it with his nose. It squeaked on dry hinges.

He froze. Waiting. Waiting.

He heard nothing. He peered inside. His gaze darted around the room.

Everywhere he looked, the low-burning candle cast flickering shadows. He turned his attention to the bed. He saw Laura's arm dangling over the edge of the mattress.

Your father is dead, Laura. You will inherit the land. You will give it to me. I will own this rich farm. The homestead my father dreamed of building for our family.

He slipped inside and padded across the room. Alert to any noises, he crept toward her bed on silent feet. He did not want to wake her. But he wanted to see her.

He rose up on his haunches and put his front paws on the bed. He looked down at her with the eyes of a wolf. He gazed at her pale skin. So incredibly white. His gaze moved to her soft mouth. Her lips were slightly parted, cast with a strange bluish hue.

He jumped onto the bed. Laura did not stir. Her eyes did not open. She simply lay there. Unmoving.

He pressed his nose to her cheek. It was cold. So cold.

He angled his head and laid it to her chest. He could hear no heartbeat. No intake of breath.

He growled low in his throat as the truth hit him.

Laura would not inherit the land! She would give nothing to Jamie.

She was dead!

Chapter
29

How did she die? Jamie wondered. Was she really as sick as she always claimed?

He nudged her cold cheek with his nose. He turned her face so he could see her throat. No bruises. No red marks. She looked untouched.

Warily, Jamie glanced around the room. He heard nothing. He saw nothing unusual. He sniffed Laura. He smelled something bitter near her mouth.

Jamie jumped off the bed. The glass was on the floor, shattered. The milk formed a creamy white pool. Jamie sniffed it. He could smell the same bitter odor.

Poison! Someone poisoned Laura.

Amanda! Jamie realized. Amanda killed her sister. Why? Because I married her?

Does she plan to kill me, too? Was her walk just an excuse to have someone load the rifle for her?

I will have to be careful. I can't let her see me. Not tonight. Not while a full moon burns in the sky.

He padded across the room and peered into the hallway. It was dark. Quiet. Where is she? he wondered. Where is Amanda hiding?

He heard a high-pitched wail. Amanda! She found her father, he realized.

I can run to the woods now, run without her seeing me. In the morning, I will return. At dawn. In my human form, she is not a threat to me. I will deal with her then.

He crept out of the room. Stealthily, he padded down the steps. The front door was closed. He had no way to open it.

He couldn't escape through the broken window in Lucien's study. Amanda would see him. And he would stay a wolf forever.

He trotted to the back of the house, to the kitchen. He would break through the window. What were a few more cuts and scrapes when the alternative was death—or worse?

He was surprised to find the back door open. Amanda must have forgotten to shut it when she went for her walk, he thought.

Soon she will go for help. I must get to the woods before they come to look for me.

He raced across the kitchen. Rushed through the back door . . . and slammed into iron bars. His foot snagged a cord. Metal grated against metal as a door made of iron bars slammed down behind him.

Jamie spun around. He saw four walls of thick iron bars on each side. He looked up. Iron bars above as well. Below his feet he saw a cold metal floor.

He twisted and paced from one side of the cage to the other. A short distance, barely the length of his wolf's body.

Trapped! Trapped in a cage, like an animal. With no way out.

"Jamie!" Amanda called.

He heard her footsteps echo down the hallway. He heard the steps grow louder. Coming closer.

Jamie backed up. Backed into the corner. He curled into a tight ball. He felt the iron bars pressing into his back.

He heard Amanda enter the kitchen. Cross over to the back door.

He didn't move a muscle. He didn't breathe.

He saw candlelight fill the doorway.

He looked up.

Amanda stood stone still, staring at him.

Chapter
30

Searing pain ripped through his body. Tore through his chest. Speared his heart.

He crumpled to the ground. His body trembled, then convulsed.

No, he thought. This can't be happening. She hasn't touched me, but it feels as though she is killing me!

Only he didn't die.

The pain increased. His muscles ballooned out . . . and settled back into place. His bones cracked.

He howled. He rolled over and over. His body slammed against the sides of the cage.

His throat tightened and he could feel his blood— pulsing, throbbing, thrumming through his veins. Cold. Then hot.

Amanda knelt in front of the cage. "Jamie, I love you."

No! Jamie screamed in his mind. *No!*

"I tried to hate you," she said. "But I couldn't. I've loved you for so long. Truly loved you."

True love!

Jamie felt his body settling into its permanent shape. Sealing the bones. Molding the muscles. Making certain that he would always be—

A wolf!

His body jerked a final time. Then became still. Breathing heavily, Jamie glared at Amanda. He growled deep within his chest.

"Don't get angry," she whispered. "I've always loved you. I've always wanted you to belong to me. I know you don't love me. But that's all right. In time, you'll come to love me because I'll take care of you."

He snarled.

"I knew you were the wolf," she told him. "The tooth you wear around your neck gave you away. It's like the tooth in the legend, and I always believed the legend."

He bared his teeth. Saliva dripped from his jaws.

"You don't have to worry. I'll take care of Papa's body. I understand why you killed him. He hurt you and your family. I won't let anyone hurt you. Ever again."

She sighed. "I know you're probably angry about Laura, and I should tell you everything. I started slowly poisoning her the night you arrived. After supper. I watched you while you ate the meal. You couldn't take your eyes off her, and I got jealous."

He growled low, a thrumming sound that made his throat vibrate.

"I know it was wrong of me," she continued, "but it was so easy to do. She always claimed to feel sick, especially when she had to do chores. So no one believed her when she really wasn't feeling well."

She inched closer to the metal bars. "I was so happy when it seemed as if you loved me, too. But when you chose Laura to be your wife, I thought I would die of the pain you caused me."

I should have killed you that day at the falls, Jamie thought. I should have killed you when I had my chance.

A chance I will never have again, he realized.

He lowered his gaze to her throat and watched her pulse, beating, beating. Pumping her thick, rich blood through her veins. Only he couldn't reach her throat through the bars. He couldn't touch her. She was safe from him.

"I'm sorry you don't love me," she said quietly. "I'm sorry that you left me no choice but to turn you into a wolf forever. It's not how I'd planned for us to remain together for the rest of our lives, but it can't be changed. Once done, it cannot be undone."

Jamie shuddered at the words he'd heard long ago—words uttered by Withering Woman.

Once done, it cannot be undone.

He remembered other words Withering Woman

had said. Only true love was strong enough to make him a wolf forever.

How can Amanda truly love me when I don't love her? he wondered.

"I know you're probably angry with me right now," Amanda said. She stepped into the doorway and put her hand on the knob. "But I told you once that someday you would belong to me."

She stepped into the kitchen, drew the door toward her, and peered through the small opening.

"And now you do belong to me. Forever."

Behind the
Iron Bars

Forever.

Her words made ice run through my veins.

Amanda closed the door. Its click echoed into the night. I began to pace.

Pace back and forth, back and forth. With no way to escape. Forever a prisoner.

Behind iron bars.

Trapped forever within the body of a wolf.

About R.L. Stine

R.L. Stine is the best-selling author in America. He has written more than one hundred scary books for young people, all of them bestsellers.

His series include *Fear Street, Ghosts of Fear Street* and the *Fear Street Sagas*.

Bob grew up in Columbus, Ohio. Today he lives in New York City with his wife, Jane, his teenage son, Matt, and his dog, Nadine.

The Fear family has many dark secrets.
The family curse has touched many lives.
Discover the truth about them all in the

FEAR STREET SAGAS

Next . . .
THE AWAKENING EVIL
(Coming mid-November)

Everyone knows the story of the Evil. The Evil that terrorized Corky Corcoran and the cheerleaders of Shadyside High. The Evil that destroyed Sarah Fear one hundred years ago.

Everyone *thinks* they know the story.

But the true story has remained hidden. Only Sarah Fear knows where the Evil began. What it wants. And why it kills.

Read Sarah's story . . . and discover the truth at last.

R.L. STINE'S
GHOSTS OF FEAR STREET ®

Simon & Schuster Mail Order
200 Old Tappan Rd., Old Tappan, N.J. 07675
Please send me the books I have checked above. I am enclosing $_____ (please add
$0.75 to cover the postage and handling for each order. Please add appropriate sales
tax). Send check or money order--no cash or C.O.D.'s please. Allow up to six weeks
for delivery. For purchase over $10.00 you may use VISA: card number, expiration
date and customer signature must be included.

POCKET
B O O K S

Name _____

Address _____

City _____ State/Zip _____

VISA Card # _____ Exp. Date _____

Signature _____

1180-21